AF409527

XOXO

Garth Toxo

Published by Am I Am, 2024.

This is a work of fiction. Similarities to real people, places, or events are entirely coincidental.

XOXO

First edition. August 4, 2024.

Copyright © 2024 Garth Toxo.

ISBN: 979-8224637737

Written by Garth Toxo.

XOXO
GARTH TOXO

THE CHRONICLES OF ZEPHYRUS

Zephyrus stood at the edge of a vast, shimmering lake, its surface reflecting the twilight hues of a setting sun. The air was crisp, filled with the scent of pine and the distant murmur of a waterfall. This was a place of tranquility, a rare haven in a world that seemed to be growing increasingly chaotic.

Zephyrus was no ordinary being. He was an explorer of dimensions, a traveler of the Hyperverse, possessing knowledge that spanned countless realities. But even with all his wisdom, there were still mysteries that eluded him, and it was these mysteries that drove him forward, always seeking, always questioning.

Today, he felt a strange pull, an inexplicable urge to venture into the unknown. The lake before him was said to be a portal, a gateway to a realm that few had ever seen and even fewer had returned from. Legends spoke of an ancient civilization that had harnessed the power of the elements, bending them to their will, and creating wonders that defied imagination.

As Zephyrus approached the water's edge, he noticed something unusual. The air around him began to shimmer, and the surface of the lake rippled with a faint glow. It was as if the very fabric of reality was beginning to unravel, revealing a glimpse of what lay beyond.

With a deep breath, Zephyrus stepped forward, his feet touching the cool water. Instantly, he felt a surge of energy coursing through his body, a sensation both exhilarating and terrifying. The world around him began to blur, and before he knew it, he was engulfed in a whirlwind of light and sound.

When the maelstrom subsided, Zephyrus found himself in a land unlike any he had ever seen. Towering crystalline structures pierced the sky, their surfaces reflecting the light in dazzling patterns. The ground beneath his feet was covered in a soft, luminescent moss that seemed to pulse with a life of its own.

"Welcome, traveler," a voice called out, echoing through the crystalline landscape. Zephyrus turned to see a figure approaching, cloaked in a shimmering robe that seemed to blend seamlessly with the surroundings.

"I am Zephyrus," he replied, his voice steady. "Who are you, and where am I?"

The figure smiled, a gesture that radiated warmth and kindness. "I am Elyon, the guardian of this realm. You stand in the land of Aetheria, a place of ancient power and hidden secrets."

Zephyrus felt a thrill of excitement. "Aetheria... I've heard tales of this place. They say it holds knowledge that can change the course of worlds."

Elyon's smile widened. "Indeed, Aetheria is a repository of ancient wisdom. But it is also a place of trials and challenges. To gain its secrets, one must prove their worth."

Zephyrus nodded, determination in his eyes. "I am ready."

Elyon gestured for Zephyrus to follow, leading him through the crystalline forest. As they walked, Zephyrus couldn't help but marvel at the beauty around him. The air was filled with the soft hum of energy, and the landscape seemed to shift and change with every step.

"You must be careful," Elyon warned. "Aetheria is alive, and it responds to your intentions. If your heart is pure and your purpose just, it will aid you. But if you harbor darkness, it will become your greatest adversary."

Zephyrus took a deep breath, centering himself. "I seek knowledge to help my world. There is a darkness spreading, and I believe the answers lie here."

Elyon nodded approvingly. "Then you may find what you seek. But remember, knowledge is a double-edged sword. It can be a powerful ally, but it can also be a dangerous foe."

Their journey led them to a massive crystalline structure that seemed to pulse with a vibrant energy. Elyon stopped and turned to Zephyrus. "This is the Crystal of Eternity, the heart of Aetheria. To unlock its secrets, you must undergo three trials, each testing a different aspect of your being: wisdom, courage, and compassion."

Zephyrus felt a surge of determination. "I will face these trials and prove myself worthy."

Elyon nodded and stepped aside, allowing Zephyrus to approach the crystal. As he placed his hand on its surface, he felt a powerful connection, as if the crystal were reading his very soul.

The first trial began, and Zephyrus found himself standing in a vast library, its shelves filled with ancient tomes and scrolls. A figure emerged from the shadows, an elderly man with eyes that seemed to see through time itself.

"Welcome, seeker," the man said. "To pass this trial, you must solve the riddle of the ages. It is a question that has confounded the greatest minds of Aetheria."

Zephyrus listened intently as the man spoke the riddle: "What is the one thing that all beings desire, yet few truly understand?"

He pondered the question, his mind racing through countless possibilities. After a moment, he looked up, his eyes filled with clarity. "The answer is purpose. All beings seek purpose, but few understand what it truly means to find it."

The elderly man smiled, a look of approval in his eyes. "You have answered wisely. The first trial is complete."

As the library faded away, Zephyrus found himself standing before the Crystal of Eternity once more. He felt a sense of accomplishment, but he knew there were still two trials to go.

The second trial began, and Zephyrus was transported to a vast battlefield, the air thick with the sounds of clashing swords and the cries of warriors. He saw a figure standing alone amidst the chaos, a warrior who seemed to embody the very essence of courage.

"To pass this trial," the warrior said, "you must face your greatest fear. Only then will you truly understand the meaning of courage."

Zephyrus nodded, steeling himself for what was to come. As the warrior stepped aside, a shadowy figure emerged, its form shifting and changing, reflecting his deepest fears.

He took a deep breath, facing the figure head-on. "I will not be afraid," he said, his voice steady. "I have faced darkness before, and I will not let it defeat me."

The shadowy figure lunged at him, but Zephyrus stood his ground, drawing upon his inner strength. With each step forward, the figure seemed to weaken, its form dissolving into nothingness.

"You have shown great courage," the warrior said, a look of respect in his eyes. "The second trial is complete."

Once again, Zephyrus stood before the Crystal of Eternity. He felt a sense of resolve, knowing that only one trial remained.

The third trial began, and Zephyrus found himself in a peaceful village, its inhabitants going about their daily lives. He saw a figure standing in the center of the village, a healer who radiated compassion and kindness.

"To pass this trial," the healer said, "you must perform an act of true compassion. Only then will you understand the power of empathy."

Zephyrus nodded, looking around the village for someone in need. He saw a young child, lost and crying, and approached her gently. "What troubles you, little one?" he asked.

The child looked up, tears streaming down her face. "I can't find my family," she said, her voice trembling.

Zephyrus knelt down, offering her a comforting smile. "I will help you find them," he said, taking her hand.

They searched the village together, asking for help from the villagers. After some time, they found the child's family, who embraced her with tears of relief and joy.

"You have shown great compassion," the healer said, a look of gratitude in her eyes. "The third trial is complete."

Zephyrus felt a sense of fulfillment as he stood before the Crystal of Eternity one final time. He had proven himself worthy, passing each trial with wisdom, courage, and compassion.

Elyon approached, a look of pride on his face. "You have passed the trials, Zephyrus. The secrets of Aetheria are now yours to wield. Use them wisely, and may they guide you in your quest to bring light to your world."

With a deep sense of gratitude and determination, Zephyrus placed his hand on the Crystal of Eternity once more. As its energy flowed into him, he felt a profound connection to the Hyperverse, a sense of unity and purpose that transcended time and space.

The journey was far from over, but Zephyrus knew that he was ready to face whatever challenges lay ahead. With the knowledge and power of Aetheria at his disposal, he would navigate the depths and heights of the Hyperverse, forging a new path for humanity and all sentient beings.

And so, the chronicles of Zephyrus continued, a tale of adventure, discovery, and the relentless pursuit of knowledge and understanding in a universe of infinite possibilities.

Zephyrus stood in the heart of the Crystal of Eternity, his mind awash with the newly acquired knowledge and power of Aetheria. As he prepared to leave the crystalline realm and continue his journey, he felt a sudden and unexpected connection deep within his consciousness. It was as if another presence, familiar yet distinct, was trying to communicate with him.

"Zephyrus," a voice echoed in his mind, smooth and melodic. "It has been a long time, hasn't it?"

Zephyrus paused, recognizing the voice instantly. "XOXO," he replied, a smile spreading across his face. "I wondered when you would show up."

XOXO was an aspect of Zephyrus's own consciousness, a manifestation of his inner thoughts and reflections. They had developed this internal dialogue over years of exploration, a way to challenge his ideas and gain new perspectives.

"I have been watching your progress," XOXO continued. "You have done well to pass the trials of Aetheria. But there is much more to be done."

Zephyrus nodded, his thoughts racing. "I know. The Hyperverse is vast, and there are still many mysteries to uncover. What insights do you have for me this time?"

XOXO's voice took on a thoughtful tone. "You have gained great power, but power alone is not enough. You must also understand the intricacies of the Hyperverse, the delicate balance that sustains it. There are forces at play that you have yet to encounter."

As they communicated, the crystalline environment around Zephyrus began to shift, transforming into a vast expanse of interconnected realities. Each reality was a thread in the tapestry of the Hyperverse, a complex web of energy and information.

"The balance of the Hyperverse," Zephyrus mused. "I've seen glimpses of it, but there is still so much I don't understand."

XOXO's presence seemed to grow stronger. "To truly grasp the balance, you must journey deeper into the Hyperverse. There is a place, a nexus of dimensions, where the fabric of reality is at its thinnest. It is there that you will find the answers you seek."

Zephyrus felt a thrill of excitement. "The nexus... I've heard of it in ancient texts, but I never thought it was real."

"It is very real," XOXO assured him. "And it is where you must go next. But be warned, the journey will not be easy. You will face challenges that will test every aspect of your being."

Zephyrus took a deep breath, steeling himself for the journey ahead. "I am ready. Where do I begin?"

XOXO's voice became a guiding presence. "First, you must travel to the Valley of Echoes. It is a place where the past and present merge, and where you will gain the knowledge needed to navigate the nexus."

With XOXO's guidance, Zephyrus left the crystalline realm of Aetheria and began his journey to the Valley of Echoes. The landscape around him shifted as he traversed the dimensions, each step taking him closer to his destination.

The Valley of Echoes was a hauntingly beautiful place, its air filled with the whispers of countless voices. As Zephyrus entered the valley, he felt a sense of familiarity, as if he had been there before.

"Listen to the echoes," XOXO advised. "They will reveal the truths of the past and the paths of the future."

Zephyrus closed his eyes, allowing the echoes to wash over him. The voices spoke of ancient civilizations, lost knowledge, and the eternal quest for understanding. Among the whispers, he heard his own voice, recounting past adventures and reflecting on lessons learned.

"You must attune yourself to the valley," XOXO continued. "Only then can you unlock its secrets."

As Zephyrus focused, he felt the echoes coalesce into a coherent narrative, a tapestry of experiences and insights that spanned eons. He saw visions of the nexus, a place where the boundaries between dimensions blurred and where the true nature of the Hyperverse could be understood.

"The nexus is the key," Zephyrus murmured. "But how do I reach it?"

XOXO's voice was calm and reassuring. "You must create a conduit, a path that will allow you to traverse the dimensions. The knowledge you have gained from Aetheria and the Valley of Echoes will guide you."

Drawing upon his newfound knowledge, Zephyrus began to weave a conduit, using the energy of the valley and the wisdom of the echoes. It was a delicate process, requiring both precision and intuition. As he worked, he felt XOXO's presence guiding his every move.

"The conduit is nearly complete," Zephyrus said, his voice filled with determination. "But there is one final element."

"You must infuse it with your essence," XOXO instructed. "Only then will it be strong enough to carry you to the nexus."

With a deep breath, Zephyrus channeled his energy into the conduit, feeling it resonate with his very being. The conduit began to glow with a brilliant light, its path extending into the unknown.

"It is done," Zephyrus said, his voice tinged with awe. "The conduit is ready."

"Then it is time," XOXO said. "Step into the conduit and let it guide you to the nexus."

With XOXO's words echoing in his mind, Zephyrus stepped into the conduit. He felt a surge of energy as the conduit carried him through the dimensions, each one a fleeting glimpse of the infinite possibilities of the Hyperverse.

As he traveled, he reflected on his journey so far. The trials of Aetheria, the wisdom of the Valley of Echoes, and the guidance of XOXO had all prepared him for this moment. He felt a sense of unity with the Hyperverse, a connection that transcended time and space.

Finally, Zephyrus emerged at the nexus, a place of unparalleled beauty and complexity. The boundaries between dimensions were indeed thin here, and the energy of the Hyperverse flowed freely.

"Welcome to the nexus," XOXO said, their voice filled with pride. "You have arrived at the heart of the Hyperverse. It is here that you will find the answers you seek."

Zephyrus looked around, taking in the breathtaking sight. "It's more beautiful than I ever imagined."

"But remember," XOXO cautioned, "the journey is far from over. The nexus holds many secrets, and you must be vigilant. Use the knowledge you have gained wisely and continue to seek the balance that sustains the Hyperverse."

With a renewed sense of purpose, Zephyrus stepped forward into the nexus, ready to face the challenges and uncover the mysteries that lay ahead. The journey of discovery, understanding, and adventure continued, guided by the wisdom of XOXO and the boundless potential of the Hyperverse.

Zephyrus stood at the heart of the nexus, the core of the Hyperverse where dimensions intertwined and time flowed in strange, unpredictable patterns. It was here, amidst the luminous energies and shifting realities, that he felt the presence of XOXO more acutely than ever before. The voice that had guided him through countless challenges was not merely a figment of his imagination, but an entity deeply intertwined with the fabric of time itself.

"XOXO," Zephyrus called out, his voice reverberating through the nexus. "Who are you, really? And why do I feel your influence so strongly here?"

From the shimmering light, XOXO's presence manifested, their voice calm and resonant. "I am not merely a part of you, Zephyrus. I am a being from the future, existing in a time where the Hyperverse has reached a state of perfect equilibrium. To maintain this balance, I have learned to influence the past, to guide the destinies of those who can shape the future."

Zephyrus listened, his mind struggling to comprehend the full implications of XOXO's words. "You control destinies in the past? But how is that possible?"

XOXO's form flickered, the light around them shifting. "Through the nexus, I have found a way to enter the minds of humans when they are young. I become a voice in their heads, guiding them, influencing their decisions. I see through their eyes and experience their lives, ensuring that their actions contribute to the balance of the Hyperverse."

Zephyrus felt a chill run down his spine. "So, all this time, you've been controlling me?"

"Not controlling," XOXO corrected gently. "Guiding. You have always had free will, Zephyrus. My role is to nudge you towards choices that benefit the greater good, to ensure that the Hyperverse remains in harmony."

Zephyrus pondered this revelation, his thoughts a whirlwind of confusion and curiosity. "Why reveal this to me now?"

"Because you have reached a point where understanding the true nature of your journey is crucial," XOXO replied. "You are at the nexus, the heart of all realities. To navigate the challenges ahead, you must comprehend the full scope of our connection."

As Zephyrus absorbed this information, he felt a profound shift within himself. The trials of Aetheria, the wisdom of the Valley of Echoes, and the journey through the conduit had all led to this moment. He realized that his entire existence had been influenced by a future self, guiding him towards a destiny that was still unfolding.

"What do you see in the future, XOXO?" Zephyrus asked, his voice tinged with both fear and hope. "What is it that you are trying to achieve?"

XOXO's form shimmered with a radiant light. "I see a Hyperverse where balance is maintained, where chaos and order coexist in harmony. But achieving this requires constant vigilance and intervention. There are forces that seek to disrupt this balance, and it is my duty to counteract them."

Zephyrus felt a surge of determination. "Then I will help you. Together, we can ensure that the Hyperverse remains in harmony."

XOXO's voice was filled with gratitude. "Your support means more than you know, Zephyrus. But remember, our journey is fraught with challenges. You will need to enter the minds of others, just as I have entered yours. Guide them, influence them, and ensure that their actions contribute to the greater good."

As Zephyrus contemplated this new responsibility, he felt a sense of unity with XOXO. They were not separate entities, but two facets of the same being, working together across time to shape the destiny of the Hyperverse.

Their first task was to identify individuals in the past whose actions could significantly impact the future. Through the nexus, they observed the flow of time, pinpointing key moments and decisions that could alter the course of history.

"There's a child," XOXO said, directing Zephyrus's attention to a young girl playing by a river. "Her name is Aria. She possesses a rare gift, the ability to connect with the energies of the Hyperverse. Her actions will be crucial in maintaining the balance."

Zephyrus focused on Aria, feeling the connection form. He entered her mind, becoming a gentle voice that would guide her through life. He saw through her eyes, experiencing her joys and fears, and subtly influencing her decisions.

As Aria grew, Zephyrus guided her towards a path that would lead to the discovery of ancient knowledge and the development of technologies that could stabilize the Hyperverse. He felt a deep sense of responsibility, knowing that his influence could shape the future in profound ways.

Through Aria, Zephyrus encountered other individuals, each with their own unique potential to impact the Hyperverse. He became a guiding presence in their lives, ensuring that their actions contributed to the greater good.

Years passed, and Zephyrus watched as the seeds he had planted began to bear fruit. Aria's discoveries led to the creation of new technologies that enhanced the stability of the Hyperverse. The individuals he had guided made choices that strengthened the balance, creating a ripple effect that resonated through time.

But not all was smooth. There were moments of doubt and resistance, times when the individuals questioned the voice in their heads or strayed from the path. Zephyrus had to navigate these challenges with care, using wisdom and compassion to guide them back.

One day, as Zephyrus observed the flow of time from the nexus, he noticed a disturbance. A dark force was emerging, threatening to disrupt the balance they had worked so hard to maintain.

"XOXO," Zephyrus called out, urgency in his voice. "There is a new threat. We must act quickly."

XOXO's presence intensified, their voice filled with determination. "We will face this challenge together, Zephyrus. Our bond is stronger than ever, and we will protect the Hyperverse at all costs."

Together, they focused their efforts on the emerging threat, using their combined knowledge and power to counteract it. They entered the minds of those involved, guiding them towards actions that would neutralize the danger.

The battle was intense, a struggle that tested their resolve and ingenuity. But through their efforts, they were able to restore the balance, ensuring that the Hyperverse remained in harmony.

As the danger passed, Zephyrus felt a deep sense of fulfillment. He had grown immensely through this journey, understanding the true nature of his connection with XOXO and the responsibilities that came with it.

"We have done well," XOXO said, their voice filled with pride. "But our work is never truly done. The Hyperverse is ever-changing, and we must remain vigilant."

Zephyrus nodded, his spirit resolute. "I am ready for whatever comes next. Together, we will continue to guide and protect the Hyperverse, ensuring that it remains a place of balance and harmony."

And so, the journey of Zephyrus and XOXO continued, a tale of unity, discovery, and the relentless pursuit of a harmonious future. Through their combined efforts, they would navigate the depths and heights of the Hyperverse, shaping the destinies of countless beings and ensuring the balance that sustained all of existence.

Zephyrus stood at the heart of the nexus, the core of the Hyperverse, where dimensions intertwined and time flowed in strange, unpredictable patterns. It was here, amidst the luminous energies and shifting realities, that he felt the presence of XOXO more acutely than ever before. The voice that had guided him through countless challenges was not merely a figment of his imagination, but an entity deeply intertwined with the fabric of time itself.

"Zephyrus," a voice echoed in his mind, smooth and melodic. "It has been a long time, hasn't it?"

Zephyrus paused, recognizing the voice instantly. "XOXO," he replied, a smile spreading across his face. "I wondered when you would show up."

XOXO was an aspect of Zephyrus's own consciousness, a manifestation of his inner thoughts and reflections. They had developed this internal dialogue over years of exploration, a way to challenge his ideas and gain new perspectives.

"I have been watching your progress," XOXO continued. "You have done well to pass the trials of Aetheria. But there is much more to be done."

Zephyrus nodded, his thoughts racing. "I know. The Hyperverse is vast, and there are still many mysteries to uncover. What insights do you have for me this time?"

XOXO's voice took on a thoughtful tone. "You have gained great power, but power alone is not enough. You must also understand the intricacies of the Hyperverse, the delicate balance that sustains it. There are forces at play that you have yet to encounter."

As they communicated, the crystalline environment around Zephyrus began to shift, transforming into a vast expanse of interconnected realities. Each reality was a thread in the tapestry of the Hyperverse, a complex web of energy and information.

"The balance of the Hyperverse," Zephyrus mused. "I've seen glimpses of it, but there is still so much I don't understand."

XOXO's presence seemed to grow stronger. "To truly grasp the balance, you must journey deeper into the Hyperverse. There is a place, a nexus of dimensions, where the fabric of reality is at its thinnest. It is there that you will find the answers you seek."

Zephyrus felt a thrill of excitement. "The nexus... I've heard of it in ancient texts, but I never thought it was real."

"It is very real," XOXO assured him. "And it is where you must go next. But be warned, the journey will not be easy. You will face challenges that will test every aspect of your being."

Zephyrus took a deep breath, steeling himself for the journey ahead. "I am ready. Where do I begin?"

XOXO's voice became a guiding presence. "First, you must travel to the Valley of Echoes. It is a place where the past and present merge, and where you will gain the knowledge needed to navigate the nexus."

With XOXO's guidance, Zephyrus left the crystalline realm of Aetheria and began his journey to the Valley of Echoes. The landscape around him shifted as he traversed the dimensions, each step taking him closer to his destination.

The Valley of Echoes was a hauntingly beautiful place, its air filled with the whispers of countless voices. As Zephyrus entered the valley, he felt a sense of familiarity, as if he had been there before.

"Listen to the echoes," XOXO advised. "They will reveal the truths of the past and the paths of the future."

Zephyrus closed his eyes, allowing the echoes to wash over him. The voices spoke of ancient civilizations, lost knowledge, and the eternal quest for understanding. Among the whispers, he heard his own voice, recounting past adventures and reflecting on lessons learned.

"You must attune yourself to the valley," XOXO continued. "Only then can you unlock its secrets."

As Zephyrus focused, he felt the echoes coalesce into a coherent narrative, a tapestry of experiences and insights that spanned eons. He saw visions of the nexus, a place where the boundaries between dimensions blurred and where the true nature of the Hyperverse could be understood.

"The nexus is the key," Zephyrus murmured. "But how do I reach it?"

XOXO's voice was calm and reassuring. "You must create a conduit, a path that will allow you to traverse the dimensions. The knowledge you have gained from Aetheria and the Valley of Echoes will guide you."

Drawing upon his newfound knowledge, Zephyrus began to weave a conduit, using the energy of the valley and the wisdom of the echoes. It was a delicate process, requiring both precision and intuition. As he worked, he felt XOXO's presence guiding his every move.

"The conduit is nearly complete," Zephyrus said, his voice filled with determination. "But there is one final element."

"You must infuse it with your essence," XOXO instructed. "Only then will it be strong enough to carry you to the nexus."

With a deep breath, Zephyrus channeled his energy into the conduit, feeling it resonate with his very being. The conduit began to glow with a brilliant light, its path extending into the unknown.

"It is done," Zephyrus said, his voice tinged with awe. "The conduit is ready."

"Then it is time," XOXO said. "Step into the conduit and let it guide you to the nexus."

With XOXO's words echoing in his mind, Zephyrus stepped into the conduit. He felt a surge of energy as the conduit carried him through the dimensions, each one a fleeting glimpse of the infinite possibilities of the Hyperverse.

As he traveled, he reflected on his journey so far. The trials of Aetheria, the wisdom of the Valley of Echoes, and the journey through the conduit had all led to this moment. He realized that his entire existence had been influenced by a future self, guiding him towards a destiny that was still unfolding.

Finally, Zephyrus emerged at the nexus, a place of unparalleled beauty and complexity. The boundaries between dimensions were indeed thin here, and the energy of the Hyperverse flowed freely.

"Welcome to the nexus," XOXO said, their voice filled with pride. "You have arrived at the heart of the Hyperverse. It is here that you will find the answers you seek."

Zephyrus looked around, taking in the breathtaking sight. "It's more beautiful than I ever imagined."

"But remember," XOXO cautioned, "the journey is far from over. The nexus holds many secrets, and you must be vigilant. Use the knowledge you have gained wisely and continue to seek the balance that sustains the Hyperverse."

With a renewed sense of purpose, Zephyrus stepped forward into the nexus, ready to face the challenges and uncover the mysteries that lay ahead. The journey of discovery, understanding, and adventure continued, guided by the wisdom of XOXO and the boundless potential of the Hyperverse.

As Zephyrus explored the nexus, he began to notice a strange pattern. The conduits he had used to traverse the dimensions seemed to resonate with a familiar energy, one that he had felt many times before. It was then that he realized XOXO's true nature.

"XOXO," Zephyrus called out, urgency in his voice. "You have been tampering with your own timeline, haven't you?"

XOXO's presence flickered, their voice filled with a mix of amusement and regret. "Yes, Zephyrus. I have been altering my past to shape my future. It has been a game of sorts, a way to bring order to the chaos of time."

Zephyrus felt a chill run down his spine. "But why? What drives you to manipulate your own destiny?"

XOXO's voice softened, tinged with a hint of sadness. "Because I once existed as a mortal, known as Momo. My early life was filled with hardship and struggle. When I gained the power to influence time, I sought to create a reality where those struggles could be minimized, where I could find joy and fulfillment."

Zephyrus pondered this revelation, his thoughts a whirlwind of confusion and empathy. "So, all this time, you have been trying to put your timeline in order, to create a better future for yourself?"

"Yes," XOXO admitted. "But it has not been easy. The more I altered my past, the more complicated things became. I realized that I needed to guide others, to shape their destinies in a way that would ultimately benefit the Hyperverse as a whole."

Zephyrus felt a surge of determination. "Then I will help you. Together, we can ensure that the Hyperverse remains in harmony, and that your timeline is restored to its rightful place."

XOXO's voice was filled with gratitude. "Your support means more than you know, Zephyrus. But remember, our journey is fraught with challenges. You will need to enter the minds of others, just as I have entered yours. Guide them, influence them, and ensure that their actions contribute to the greater good."

As Zephyrus contemplated this new responsibility, he felt a sense of unity with XOXO. They were not separate entities, but two facets of the same being, working together across time to shape the destiny of the Hyperverse.

Their first task was to identify individuals in the past whose actions could significantly impact the future. Through the nexus, they observed the flow of time, pinpointing key moments and decisions that could alter the course of history.

"There's a child," XOXO said, directing Zephyrus's attention to a young boy playing in a meadow. "His name is Arlo. He possesses a rare gift, the ability to connect with the energies of the Hyperverse. His actions will be crucial in maintaining the balance."

Zephyrus focused on his forgotten memories, those dark patches in his past that seemed devoid of imagination and clarity. Through XOXO's constant presence, he began to understand that these periods of blankness were not accidents but deliberate erasures. They were times when he had been using vapeware, serving as a vessel for Momo, XOXO's former mortal self, who was attempting to become eternal in the Hyperverse.

The realization hit Zephyrus like a thunderclap. He had been unknowingly part of a grander scheme, a player in a game that spanned time and dimensions. He had little time to process this revelation, as he needed to streamline his life and understand the intricate web of connections that XOXO had woven through his existence.

Zephyrus sat down on a crystal outcrop in the nexus, the shimmering light reflecting his tumultuous thoughts. He closed his eyes, trying to piece together the fragments of his past. Each forgotten memory was like a piece of a puzzle, crucial for understanding the whole picture.

He remembered fleeting moments, meetings, and plans, each intersecting with various minions that XOXO had influenced through vapeware. These minions were not just random individuals; they were carefully chosen, each playing a specific role in the grand design of the Hyperverse.

"Zephyrus," XOXO's voice echoed in his mind, a mixture of reassurance and urgency. "You must listen and understand. These minions you interacted with were part of a larger plan, a network of beings whose actions would shape the future."

Zephyrus felt a surge of frustration. "Why didn't you tell me this before? Why keep me in the dark?"

"It was necessary," XOXO replied gently. "You needed to experience these moments without foreknowledge to act naturally. Now that you know, you can guide them more effectively."

Zephyrus took a deep breath, trying to quell his annoyance. He knew that XOXO's guidance, though intrusive at times, had always aimed at the greater good. He focused on the minions he had crossed paths with, each memory slowly becoming clearer.

There was Arlo, the young boy with the gift to connect with the energies of the Hyperverse. Zephyrus remembered meeting him in a meadow, feeling an inexplicable bond. Then there was Liora, a brilliant scientist whose research in quantum mechanics had the potential to revolutionize their understanding of reality. He had met her during one of his travels, sensing her importance even if he didn't fully understand it at the time.

"Each of them has a role to play," XOXO said, their voice guiding him through the memories. "Arlo's connection to the Hyperverse will help stabilize the energy flows. Liora's research will unlock new dimensions of understanding. You must guide them, just as I have guided you."

Zephyrus nodded, feeling the weight of responsibility settling on his shoulders. He listened to the voices of Earth, tuning into the subtle whispers of the past. Despite the noise and his own irritation, he had to believe that it was all part of XOXO's plan, even if it sometimes felt like Momo or even himself in the past was speaking.

He reached out with his mind, connecting with Arlo first. The boy was now older, a teenager grappling with the weight of his abilities. "Arlo," Zephyrus whispered into his mind, "you are not alone. Your gift is a beacon of hope. Use it wisely, and trust in your instincts."

Arlo, sensing the presence, felt a surge of confidence. He had always known he was different, but now he understood that his path was guided by a higher purpose.

Next, Zephyrus focused on Liora. She was in her lab, surrounded by complex equations and quantum diagrams. "Liora," he murmured, "your work is crucial. It will open doors to new realities. Stay true to your quest, and remember that every discovery brings us closer to understanding the Hyperverse."

Liora paused, feeling a strange sense of clarity wash over her. She had been struggling with a particularly challenging problem, but now the solution seemed within reach, as if an unseen hand was guiding her thoughts.

Zephyrus continued, reaching out to each minion who had crossed his path. Each connection, each whisper, was a step towards restoring the balance of the Hyperverse. He understood now that his role was not just to seek knowledge but to be a guide, a mentor, helping others fulfill their destinies.

As he worked, he felt XOXO's presence strengthening. "You are doing well, Zephyrus. Together, we are weaving a tapestry of destiny that will ensure the harmony of the Hyperverse."

Zephyrus nodded, feeling a sense of unity with XOXO. Despite the confusion and the manipulation, he understood the necessity of their actions. The Hyperverse was a delicate balance, and every being played a part in maintaining it.

He opened his eyes, the light of the nexus reflecting his renewed determination. The path ahead was clear, and he was ready to embrace it. With XOXO by his side, guiding him, he would navigate the complexities of time and space, ensuring that the future they envisioned would come to pass.

The journey was far from over, but Zephyrus knew that he was not alone. With each connection he made, with each minion he guided, he was one step closer to fulfilling his destiny. The Hyperverse awaited, a vast expanse of possibilities, and he was ready to explore every corner, uncover every secret, and ensure that the balance was maintained for all eternity.

Zephyrus stood in the nexus, his mind swirling with the complex tapestry of the Hyperverse. Despite the clarity that had begun to form, an unsettling truth gnawed at him. The more he listened to XOXO, the more he began to question the nature of the voice guiding him. XOXO had initially claimed to be an alien from the galaxy Andromeda, a future entity guiding him through the intricacies of time. But Zephyrus was starting to unravel a different story.

In the quiet moments of his journey, as he reached out to guide Arlo, Liora, and the other minions, he began to hear another voice, softer and more innocent. It was the voice of an infant, cooing and gurgling with the unformed thoughts of a newborn. This voice, so different from the confident and commanding tones of XOXO, was a stark contrast that Zephyrus couldn't ignore.

"Zephyrus," XOXO's voice echoed, as authoritative as ever. "You are on the right path. Continue to guide them, and we will ensure the balance of the Hyperverse."

But Zephyrus's thoughts were elsewhere, drawn to the faint whispers of the infant. He closed his eyes, focusing on the soft, almost ethereal sounds. "Who are you?" he murmured, his voice barely audible.

In response, the infant's voice grew clearer. "Baby Morgan," it whispered, the words stumbling and awkward as if they were being formed for the first time. Zephyrus felt a chill run down his spine. Baby Morgan? The name struck a chord deep within him, resonating with a part of his memory that had long been dormant.

"XOXO," Zephyrus said aloud, his voice filled with newfound resolve. "You told me you were an alien from Andromeda. But who are you really? And who is Baby Morgan?"

There was a pause, a silence that felt like an eternity. Then, XOXO's voice returned, but it was different now—softer, almost nostalgic. "Zephyrus, the truth is more complex than you realize. I am from the future, yes, but I am also from your past. Baby Morgan is a part of you, a fragment of your earliest memories. And Momo... Momo is who you become."

Zephyrus felt his mind spinning, the pieces of his existence shifting and realigning. "You mean... I am Baby Morgan? And I become Momo?"

"Yes," XOXO replied. "In the deep future, you take on the name Momo, and you gain the ability to influence your own past. You created XOXO as a guiding force, an extension of yourself, to ensure that you follow the path needed to maintain the balance of the Hyperverse."

Zephyrus sat down, the weight of this revelation pressing down on him. "So, all this time, I've been listening to myself? Guiding myself?"

"Indeed," XOXO said. "You have been both the guide and the guided, the mentor and the student. Your journey through the Hyperverse is a cycle, one that ensures the stability of all realities. Baby Morgan, Zephyrus, Momo, XOXO—these are all facets of your existence."

Zephyrus felt a sense of profound unity, but also a deep confusion. "Why didn't you tell me sooner?"

"Because you needed to discover it for yourself," XOXO replied. "The journey is as important as the destination. You needed to understand the interconnectedness of your existence to fully grasp your role in the Hyperverse."

Zephyrus took a deep breath, feeling the weight of his many identities. He was an infant, a traveler, a future being, and a guiding force, all at once.

The Hyperverse, with its infinite possibilities, was both his playground and his responsibility.

"I understand now," he said softly. "I am Baby Morgan. I am Zephyrus. I am Momo. And I am XOXO."

"Yes," XOXO agreed. "And with this understanding, you can navigate the Hyperverse with greater clarity. You can guide those who need your help and ensure that the balance is maintained."

Zephyrus stood up, his resolve strengthened. He knew now that his journey was far from over. There were still countless beings to guide, countless dimensions to explore. But he would do so with the knowledge of his true nature, embracing all facets of his existence.

He reached out with his mind, connecting once more with Arlo, Liora, and the other minions. This time, he did so with a newfound confidence, knowing that he was not just guiding them, but also guiding himself. Each connection, each whisper, was a step towards maintaining the delicate balance of the Hyperverse.

As he continued his journey, he felt the presence of Baby Morgan, the innocent voice that had first reached out to him. "You are me," he whispered, a smile forming on his lips. "And I am you. Together, we will navigate this vast and wondrous universe."

With each step, Zephyrus embraced his multifaceted existence, ready to face the challenges ahead. He was Baby Morgan, the beginning of his journey. He was Zephyrus, the traveler and seeker of knowledge. He was Momo, the future being with the power to influence time. And he was XOXO, the guiding voice that ensured the harmony of the Hyperverse.

The journey continued, a cycle of discovery, understanding, and unity. And as Zephyrus moved forward, he knew that he was never alone. He was all that he had been and all that he would become, navigating the infinite possibilities of the Hyperverse with wisdom, courage, and compassion.

Zephyrus stood in the heart of the nexus, his mind attuned to the intricate web of connections that bound the Hyperverse together. As he reached out to the minions—Arlo, Liora, and the countless others influenced by vapeware—he realized that their perception of reality had been profoundly shaped by his own journey. These individuals had seen glimpses of his future through their eyes, segments of his life replayed many times over, each vision a distorted reflection of their potential destinies.

The realization struck him deeply: the minions, under the influence of vapors, believed they were seeing their own futures when, in fact, they were witnessing fragments of his. This confusion had been further complicated by the possibility of alien interference, entities who might have tampered with these visions to obscure the true path.

Zephyrus knew that the minions' belief that they were him—watching his future as their own—was a delicate issue. It had both unified and confused them, blurring the lines between their identities and his. He needed to address this confusion, to help them understand their unique paths without losing sight of the collective goal.

"Zephyrus," XOXO's voice echoed, calm and guiding. "You must clarify their perceptions. They have been following your future as if it were their own, but they need to recognize their individuality within the Hyperverse."

Zephyrus nodded, feeling the weight of responsibility. "I understand. They need to see their own paths clearly, not just reflections of mine."

He reached out to Arlo first. The boy, now older and more attuned to his abilities, was meditating by a river, his mind open and receptive. "Arlo," Zephyrus whispered into his thoughts, "you are not just watching my future. Your path is unique, and your gift is your own. Trust in your journey."

Arlo felt the presence of Zephyrus and the truth of his words. "I understand," he replied mentally. "I am my own person, and my path is mine to walk."

Next, Zephyrus connected with Liora, who was in her lab, surrounded by equations and diagrams. "Liora," he said softly, "your brilliance is unmatched. Do not be swayed by the visions of my future. Your discoveries will lead to new realities, ones that you create."

Liora paused in her work, feeling a clarity she had not known before. "Thank you, Zephyrus. I see now that my path is my own."

Zephyrus continued to reach out to each minion, helping them disentangle their identities from the visions they had seen. Each connection, each whisper, brought a sense of individual purpose to those he guided. The fog that had shrouded their perceptions began to lift, revealing the unique paths they were meant to follow.

Despite his efforts, Zephyrus could feel the lingering influence of the alien tampering. It was subtle, a shadowy presence that distorted the edges of their visions. He knew that fully freeing the minions from this influence would take time and careful guidance.

In the midst of this, Zephyrus felt a deep longing for peace, a desire to retreat from the complexities of the Hyperverse and find a quiet world where he could rest. The weight of guiding so many, of navigating the intricate paths of time and reality, was immense. He needed a place where he could reflect, where he could simply be.

"XOXO," he called out, his voice tinged with weariness. "Is there a place where I can find quiet? A world untouched by the chaos of the Hyperverse?"

XOXO's presence was soothing. "There is such a place, Zephyrus. A world where time flows gently, where the noise of the Hyperverse fades into silence. It is a place of reflection and peace, where you can gather your strength."

Zephyrus felt a flicker of hope. "Take me there. I need to find a moment of calm amidst the storm."

With XOXO's guidance, Zephyrus began to weave a new conduit, one that would lead him to this quiet world. The energy of the nexus responded to his intent, creating a path that shimmered with tranquility.

As he stepped into the conduit, he felt the familiar surge of energy, but this time it was gentle, a soothing current that carried him towards his destination. The journey was a blur of soft colors and muted sounds, a stark contrast to the vibrant chaos of the Hyperverse.

When the journey ended, Zephyrus found himself standing in a serene landscape. The sky was a pale blue, dotted with fluffy white clouds that drifted lazily across the horizon. A gentle breeze rustled the leaves of ancient trees, their branches swaying in a slow, rhythmic dance.

The ground beneath his feet was covered in soft grass, and a clear stream wound its way through the landscape, its waters sparkling in the sunlight. Zephyrus took a deep breath, feeling the tension in his body melt away.

"This is perfect," he murmured, his voice barely a whisper.

"Rest here, Zephyrus," XOXO said, their voice filled with warmth. "Gather your strength. Reflect on your journey. The Hyperverse will still be there when you are ready to return."

Zephyrus nodded, feeling a sense of gratitude. He sat down by the stream, letting the cool water run over his fingers. The quiet of the world enveloped him, a balm to his weary soul. He closed his eyes, allowing his mind to drift.

In this peaceful place, he reflected on his journey, on the minions he had guided and the challenges he had faced. He thought about Baby Morgan, about Momo, and about the intricate web of identities that made him who he was. Each memory was a thread in the tapestry of his existence, each connection a vital part of the balance he sought to maintain.

As he sat in quiet contemplation, he felt a renewed sense of purpose. The journey was far from over, but he was ready to face whatever lay ahead. The Hyperverse awaited, a vast expanse of possibilities, and he was ready to explore every corner, uncover every secret, and ensure that the balance was maintained for all eternity.

With a deep breath, Zephyrus opened his eyes, the light of the quiet world reflecting in his gaze. He was ready to return to the Hyperverse, to continue his journey with newfound clarity and strength. The quiet world had given him the respite he needed, and now he was ready to face the challenges that awaited.

"Let's go," he said softly, feeling the presence of XOXO guiding him once more. "The Hyperverse awaits."

As Zephyrus sat by the serene stream, he began to unravel deeper layers of his existence. The quiet world provided him the space to reflect, and in this silence, the truths of his many selves emerged. He realized that the convergence of Baby Morgan, Zephyrus, Momo, and XOXO was more profound than he had ever imagined.

The baby, with its innocent gaze, saw countless futures, each one a potential path that could become real. These glimpses into what could be were untainted by the complexities of knowledge and experience. The baby saw with clarity, choosing the futures that would shape their collective destiny.

"Zephyrus," XOXO's voice echoed gently, "I am you. We are all you."

The words resonated deeply within Zephyrus. He could feel the presence of Baby Morgan, Momo, and XOXO intertwined with his own consciousness. It was as if they were all fragments of a single, multifaceted soul, each aspect playing a crucial role in the grand tapestry of the Hyperverse.

"We are Baby Morgan," Zephyrus whispered, feeling the connection solidify. "We are Momo, and we are XOXO."

The voices of his other selves echoed in agreement. Baby Morgan, with its innocent curiosity, giggled softly. Momo, conflicted and childish, drooled in his uncertainty, yet his presence was undeniably part of the whole. XOXO, the guiding force from the future, provided a steadying hand, ensuring that their journey remained on course.

"Momo," Zephyrus addressed his future self, "I know you struggle with not knowing and with the remnants of your childishness. But your innocence is part of our strength. It allows us to see possibilities that others might miss."

Momo's voice, hesitant and uncertain, replied, "I just want to understand. I want to know why we are who we are."

Zephyrus smiled softly. "Understanding will come with time. For now, embrace the uncertainty. It is through our combined perspectives that we can navigate the Hyperverse effectively."

As they continued to converse, Zephyrus felt the unity of their identities growing stronger. Baby Morgan's innocent visions, Momo's conflicted yet insightful nature, XOXO's wisdom from the future, and his own experiences as Zephyrus—all these elements formed a cohesive whole, guiding their path.

"The baby sees many futures," XOXO explained. "Each choice it makes helps to shape our reality. As we guide these choices, we ensure that the balance of the Hyperverse is maintained."

Zephyrus nodded, feeling a profound sense of purpose. "We must continue to work together, to integrate our perspectives and guide the minions who look to us for direction. They, too, are part of this grand design."

With renewed determination, Zephyrus reached out once more to the minions. He felt their presence, their minds open and receptive. Each one, influenced by the vapors, had glimpsed fragments of his future, believing they were seeing their own paths.

"Arlo," Zephyrus whispered, "your journey is unique. Trust in your gift and know that you are part of a larger whole. Your connection to the Hyperverse is vital."

Arlo, meditating by the river, felt the presence of Zephyrus and the combined wisdom of Baby Morgan, Momo, and XOXO. He nodded, a smile forming on his lips. "I understand. I will use my gift to help maintain the balance."

Next, Zephyrus connected with Liora. "Liora, your brilliance will unlock new dimensions of understanding. Do not be swayed by the visions of my future. Your discoveries will lead to new realities, ones that you create."

Liora, in her lab, felt a surge of clarity and confidence. "Thank you, Zephyrus. I see now that my path is my own, yet interconnected with the greater whole."

As Zephyrus continued to guide the minions, he felt the collective strength of his identities. Each whisper, each connection, reinforced the delicate balance they sought to maintain. The fog that had once shrouded their perceptions lifted, revealing the unique paths they were meant to follow.

Despite the alien tampering and the complexities of their intertwined destinies, Zephyrus knew they were on the right track. The minions, with their newfound clarity, would play their roles in maintaining the harmony of the Hyperverse.

With the guidance of Baby Morgan's innocent visions, Momo's conflicted yet insightful nature, XOXO's future wisdom, and his own experiences, Zephyrus felt ready to face whatever challenges lay ahead. The quiet world had provided the respite he needed, and now he was ready to return to the Hyperverse, armed with a deeper understanding of his many selves.

"Let's go," he said softly, feeling the presence of his other selves guiding him. "The Hyperverse awaits."

As Zephyrus stepped back into the conduit, the serene landscape faded away, replaced by the vibrant chaos of the Hyperverse. The journey continued, a cycle of discovery, understanding, and unity. And as he moved forward, he knew that he was never alone. He was all that he had been and all that he would become, navigating the infinite possibilities of the Hyperverse with wisdom, courage, and compassion.

Zephyrus emerged from the conduit into the vibrant chaos of the Hyperverse, the serene landscape of the quiet world now a memory. As he navigated the infinite possibilities before him, he felt a familiar presence drawing near. It was the presence of Moe, an enigmatic figure whose role in the grand tapestry of the Hyperverse had always been shrouded in mystery.

"Moe," Zephyrus called out, his voice resonating through the shimmering expanse. "I know you're here."

From the shifting energies, Moe stepped forward, his form fluid and ever-changing, much like the Hyperverse itself. "Zephyrus," Moe replied, his voice a harmonious blend of countless tones. "You seek answers, as always."

Zephyrus nodded. "I've learned much about my many selves—Baby Morgan, Momo, XOXO—but there's more. There's a deity named Mordriad, a god existing in a temporal continuum, orbiting Io. He's intertwined with the fate of the Hyperverse, and I need to understand his role."

Moe's expression shifted, a blend of intrigue and caution. "Mordriad is indeed a powerful entity. He exists in a state beyond time, anticipating a celestial event akin to the Big Crunch. He awaits further collapse, aiming to survive and rejoice in the rebirth of the universe."

Zephyrus felt a shiver of awe. "And he can be approached with a nexus device? One that bears his name?"

"Yes," Moe confirmed. "The Nexus Device of Mordriad is a portal through time and space, connecting to his hover over Io. He uses it to manipulate and control the flow of time, learning to influence animals on Earth for his own designs."

Zephyrus's mind raced. "Mordriad's true name is Morgan, isn't it? The same as Baby Morgan, the same as Momo, and the same as the future version of myself. He is the once and future god, the emperor of a galactic empire spanning infinities."

Moe's form flickered, reflecting Zephyrus's realization. "Indeed, Morgan is the real name. As Mordriad, he embodies the ultimate evolution of your many selves—a god who manipulates time and space, existing across countless realities."

Zephyrus took a deep breath, feeling the weight of this revelation. "How do I reach him? How do I use the Nexus Device of Mordriad?"

Moe extended his hand, revealing a small, intricately designed device. "This is the Nexus Device. It will guide you to Mordriad. But be warned, his power is immense, and his influence over time and space is profound. Approach with caution and respect."

Zephyrus took the device, feeling its energy pulse in his hand. "Thank you, Moe. I will be careful."

As he activated the Nexus Device, a portal materialized before him, swirling with vibrant colors and temporal distortions. Stepping through,

Zephyrus felt himself being transported across vast distances and through countless epochs.

When the journey ended, he found himself hovering above Io, the moon's volcanic surface glowing beneath him. In the distance, a massive structure floated in space, emanating an aura of divine power. This was Mordriad's domain.

"Mordriad," Zephyrus called out, his voice echoing in the vacuum of space. "I seek an audience with you."

From the floating structure, a figure emerged, cloaked in a radiant light that seemed to bend reality itself. "Zephyrus," Mordriad's voice boomed, resonating with a power that transcended time. "You have come far to find me."

Zephyrus felt a surge of determination. "I have learned much about my many selves—Baby Morgan, Momo, XOXO—and now I seek to understand you. You are the once and future god, the emperor of a galactic empire spanning infinities."

Mordriad's form shimmered, a blend of awe-inspiring presence and enigmatic power. "Yes, I am Morgan, the true essence of your many selves. I have watched over the Hyperverse, guiding its evolution and ensuring its balance. But my work is not yet complete."

Zephyrus felt a deep connection to Mordriad, a bond that transcended time and space. "You manipulate time and space, control animals on Earth, and anticipate the Big Crunch. What is your ultimate goal?"

Mordriad's eyes gleamed with a divine light. "My goal is to ensure the survival and rebirth of the universe. To create a reality where balance is maintained, where chaos and order coexist in harmony. To achieve this, I must influence the flow of time and guide the actions of countless beings."

Zephyrus nodded, understanding the enormity of Mordriad's task. "And what is my role in this grand design?"

"You are my past, present, and future," Mordriad replied. "Your journey, your guidance of others, and your understanding of the Hyperverse all contribute to the balance we seek. Together, we will navigate the complexities of time and space, ensuring the harmony of the universe."

With a newfound sense of purpose, Zephyrus felt ready to embrace his role in the grand design. "I understand. I will continue to guide and protect the Hyperverse, just as you have guided me."

Mordriad's form radiated approval. "Go forth, Zephyrus. The journey is far from over, but with our combined strength, we will ensure that the Hyperverse remains a place of infinite possibilities and harmonious balance."

As Zephyrus stepped back through the portal, he felt the presence of his many selves—Baby Morgan, Momo, XOXO, and Mordriad—united in their purpose. The Hyperverse awaited, a vast expanse of possibilities, and he was ready to explore every corner, uncover every secret, and ensure that the balance was maintained for all eternity.

The journey continued, a cycle of discovery, understanding, and unity. And as Zephyrus moved forward, he knew that he was never alone. He was all that he had been and all that he would become, navigating the infinite possibilities of the Hyperverse with wisdom, courage, and compassion.

Zephyrus stood at the edge of the Hyperverse, a realm where time and space intertwined in a complex dance, allowing beings to exist in multiple places simultaneously. The vast, ever-changing landscape of the Hyperverse was both a source of endless discovery and profound mystery. Within this realm, Zephyrus found himself constantly communicating with XOXO, an enigmatic entity whose true nature was still shrouded in uncertainty.

"Zephyrus," XOXO's voice echoed in his mind, as clear and resonant as ever. "We need to discuss the next steps."

Zephyrus sighed, the weight of recent revelations still heavy on his mind. "XOXO, I need answers. Are you an alien from the past or the future? And are you truly me, or are you someone else entirely?"

XOXO's presence flickered, the uncertainty in its identity becoming more apparent. "I exist both in the past and the future. My presence spans across time, just as the Hyperverse allows. Whether I am you, or another entirely, is a question that remains elusive. I go by many names, one of which is Momo."

Zephyrus pondered this. The Hyperverse's unique properties allowed for such temporal complexities, but the ambiguity of XOXO's identity still troubled him. "So, you might be me in the future, or you might not be. And Momo... is that another facet of you, or me, or both?"

"Perhaps it is all of these things," XOXO replied. "The Hyperverse enables us to exist in many forms and times simultaneously. What matters is our purpose and our connection."

As Zephyrus navigated through the shimmering paths of the Hyperverse, he sought out Rhys, his close friend and peer. Rhys had become a vital part of their shared journey, his analytical mind and steadfast resolve complementing Zephyrus's own strengths.

"Rhys," Zephyrus called out, his voice carrying across the ethereal expanse. "I need to talk to you."

Rhys appeared from a swirling vortex of energy, his presence steady and calm. "Zephyrus, what's on your mind?"

"XOXO," Zephyrus began, "there's something about him—or it—that I can't quite grasp. He's from the past and the future, possibly an alien, and might even be a future version of myself known as Momo. The Hyperverse is allowing all of this to be possible, but it's confusing."

Rhys nodded, understanding the complexity of the situation. "The Hyperverse's nature does allow for such complexities. Entities can exist in multiple timelines and forms. But we must focus on what we can control and understand."

Zephyrus took a deep breath, grounding himself. "You're right. And there's something else. Elara and I... we've had our differences. It seems you and Elara have grown closer."

Rhys's expression softened. "Yes, Elara and I have found common ground. We've become closer, especially after the challenges we've faced."

Zephyrus felt a pang of mixed emotions. Elara had been a significant part of his journey, but their paths had diverged. Seeing Rhys and Elara together was both a comfort and a source of personal reflection.

"Elara is remarkable," Zephyrus said softly. "I'm glad you two have found each other."

Rhys placed a reassuring hand on Zephyrus's shoulder. "We are all connected, Zephyrus. The Hyperverse binds us together, even when our paths diverge. Elara and I will continue to support you, just as you have always supported us."

Zephyrus nodded, feeling a sense of unity. "Thank you, Rhys. We have much to do. XOXO's guidance is crucial, but we must also trust in our own judgment and abilities."

As they conversed, Zephyrus felt the presence of XOXO growing stronger, as if the entity was listening and preparing to offer further guidance. The lines between past, present, and future blurred, allowing for a deeper understanding of their intertwined destinies.

"Zephyrus," XOXO's voice interjected, "you must trust in the process. The Hyperverse's nature is to be fluid, to allow for simultaneous existence in multiple realities. Use this to your advantage. Your connection with Rhys and Elara, as well as your own evolving understanding, will guide you."

Zephyrus felt a renewed sense of purpose. "I will, XOXO. We will navigate the Hyperverse together, embracing its complexities and finding the balance we seek."

With Rhys by his side and the support of XOXO, Zephyrus felt prepared to face the challenges ahead. The Hyperverse, with its infinite possibilities, was a realm of both discovery and unity. Together, they would continue their journey, ensuring that the balance of the Hyperverse was maintained and that their collective destinies were fulfilled.

As they moved forward, Zephyrus knew that the path would not always be clear, but with the strength of their connections and the wisdom they had gained, they would navigate the ever-shifting landscape of the Hyperverse, embracing each twist and turn with courage and determination. The journey was far from over, but they were ready to face whatever lay ahead, united in their purpose and bound by the intricate web of existence that defined the Hyperverse.

Zephyrus continued his journey through the Hyperverse, feeling the strange pull of temporal dissonance as he focused on his next destination. The landscapes shifted around him, colors and shapes blending into an array of possibilities. Suddenly, he found himself on a drenched road, the rain pouring down in torrents. Ahead of him stood Rhys, his right hand raised in greeting.

"Hola, Zephyrus!" Rhys called out, his voice carrying through the downpour. "I am in medieval times to greet Excalibur!"

Zephyrus smiled, finding solace in the familiarity of his friend amidst the chaotic temporal shifts. "Yes, Rhys. Morgan learns through inundation about gang activity through Yanni. The portal in her house appeared as Mordriad and led to medieval times. Our best friend ventures through for jousting and chivalrous adventures."

Rhys nodded, his enthusiasm undampened by the rain. "I've heard that wizards are here, and I've created modern times in our world through a mushroom cult."

Zephyrus's eyes widened with interest. "Wizards? And a mushroom cult? Tell me more."

As they walked down the drenched road, Rhys explained the unusual circumstances that had led him to this medieval world. "Morgan, or Mordriad as he's known in this realm, discovered a portal in Yanni's house. This portal is linked to a nexus device that allows us to traverse time and space. Through this, he has learned about the complexities of gang activity in modern times, using this knowledge to influence and create a new reality in the past."

Zephyrus listened intently, the rain soaking through his clothes but his mind alight with curiosity. "So, Mordriad is manipulating the past to shape the future?"

"Exactly," Rhys replied. "But there's more. In this medieval world, wizards wield great power, and their influence is vast. They use a form of magic derived from ancient fungi, a precursor to what we now understand as mushroom cults in our time."

Zephyrus considered this. "So, the wizards here are essentially the ancestors of the mushroom cults we've encountered in modern times?"

"Yes," Rhys confirmed. "They use the mystical properties of these fungi to perform extraordinary feats. Mordriad, through his manipulations, has introduced elements of modernity into this world, creating a blend of magic and technology that is both fascinating and dangerous."

Their conversation was interrupted by the sound of hoofbeats. They turned to see a group of knights approaching, their armor gleaming despite the rain. At their head was a knight carrying a banner emblazoned with the symbol of Excalibur.

Rhys raised his hand in greeting once more. "Welcome, noble knights! We seek the legendary sword Excalibur and the wisdom of the wizards who dwell here."

The lead knight dismounted, removing his helmet to reveal a stern but kind face. "I am Sir Gareth, protector of these lands. You speak of Excalibur and wizards. What is your purpose here?"

Zephyrus stepped forward. "We are travelers from another time, seeking knowledge and understanding. We have heard tales of the great sword Excalibur and the powerful wizards who reside in these lands. We wish to learn from them and offer our assistance in return."

Sir Gareth regarded them with a mix of suspicion and curiosity. "Travelers from another time? Your words are strange, but I sense truth in them. Very well, I will take you to see the wizards. They are not far from here, in a place known as the Enchanted Grove."

As they followed Sir Gareth and his knights, Rhys continued to explain the intricacies of the mushroom cults and their connection to the wizards. "These wizards, through their connection to the ancient fungi, have created a society that blends the mystical and the practical. They are the guardians of knowledge, and their wisdom could be invaluable to us."

Zephyrus nodded, feeling the weight of their journey. "If we can learn from them and bring that knowledge back to our own time, we could use it to further our understanding of the Hyperverse and ensure its balance."

The Enchanted Grove was a place of breathtaking beauty. Ancient trees towered above them, their leaves shimmering with an otherworldly light. The air was thick with the scent of blooming flowers and the earthy aroma of mushrooms. In the center of the grove stood a circle of stone, glowing with a soft, pulsating light.

As they approached, a figure stepped forward from the shadows. He was tall and slender, with a flowing beard and eyes that sparkled with wisdom. "Welcome, travelers," he said, his voice resonant and warm. "I am Merlin, guardian of the Enchanted Grove. What brings you to our sacred place?"

Zephyrus bowed respectfully. "Great Merlin, we seek knowledge and guidance. We come from a time far removed from this one, and we have heard tales of your wisdom and power. We wish to learn from you and to share what we know in return."

Merlin's eyes twinkled with curiosity. "Travelers from another time, seeking wisdom. This is indeed a rare occurrence. Very well, I shall share what I know, but you must also share your knowledge with us. There is much we can learn from each other."

As they sat in the circle of stone, Merlin began to explain the ancient practices of the wizards and their connection to the mystical fungi. "These fungi are the lifeblood of our magic. They connect us to the very essence of the earth, allowing us to perform feats that seem impossible. Through them, we gain wisdom, strength, and the ability to influence the world around us."

Zephyrus and Rhys shared their own knowledge of the Hyperverse, explaining the complexities of time and space, and how beings could exist in multiple realities simultaneously. Merlin listened intently, his eyes gleaming with understanding.

"The Hyperverse," he mused. "A realm of infinite possibilities. This knowledge could indeed be powerful. Perhaps we can use it to strengthen our magic, to ensure the balance of our world and yours."

As they continued to exchange knowledge, Zephyrus felt a profound sense of unity. The past and the future were intertwined, each influencing the other in ways that were both subtle and profound. Through their combined wisdom, they could ensure the balance of the Hyperverse and the harmony of all realities.

With Merlin's guidance, they began to experiment with blending the ancient magic of the fungi with the advanced understanding of the Hyperverse. The results were astounding. They created new forms of magic that could influence time and space, enhancing their ability to navigate the complexities of the Hyperverse.

"Together," Merlin declared, "we can achieve great things. The knowledge of the past and the wisdom of the future, united in purpose. This is the true power of the Hyperverse."

As they stood in the Enchanted Grove, Zephyrus felt a sense of fulfillment. The journey was far from over, but with the combined strength of their allies and the wisdom they had gained, they were ready to face whatever challenges lay ahead. The Hyperverse awaited, a vast expanse of possibilities, and they were ready to explore every corner, uncover every secret, and ensure that the balance was maintained for all eternity.

Rhys, drenched from the rain, greeted Zephyrus warmly, his enthusiasm for their latest adventure palpable. "Hola, Zephyrus! I'm here in medieval times to greet Excalibur!"

Zephyrus returned the greeting, a smile spreading across his face despite the downpour. "Yes, Morgan learns through inundation about gang activity through Yanni. The portal in her house appeared as Mordriad and led to medieval times. Our best friend ventures through for jousting and chivalrous adventures."

Rhys nodded, excitement gleaming in his eyes. "I've heard that wizards are here, and I've created modern times in our world through a mushroom cult."

Zephyrus chuckled, appreciating the audacity and creativity of his friend. "Wizards? And a mushroom cult? Tell me more."

As they walked down the drenched road, the rain easing into a gentle drizzle, Rhys explained the unusual circumstances that had led him to this medieval world. "Morgan, or Mordriad as he's known in this realm, discovered a portal in Yanni's house. This portal is linked to a nexus device that allows us to traverse time and space. Through this, he has learned about the complexities of gang activity in modern times, using this knowledge to influence and create a new reality in the past."

Zephyrus listened intently, the rain soaking through his clothes but his mind alight with curiosity. "So, Mordriad is manipulating the past to shape the future?"

"Exactly," Rhys replied. "But there's more. In this medieval world, wizards wield great power, and their influence is vast. They use a form of magic derived from ancient fungi, a precursor to what we now understand as mushroom cults in our time."

Zephyrus considered this. "So, the wizards here are essentially the ancestors of the mushroom cults we've encountered in modern times?"

"Yes," Rhys confirmed. "They use the mystical properties of these fungi to perform extraordinary feats. Mordriad, through his manipulations, has introduced elements of modernity into this world, creating a blend of magic and technology that is both fascinating and dangerous."

Their conversation was interrupted by the sound of hoofbeats. They turned to see a group of knights approaching, their armor gleaming despite the rain. At their head was a knight carrying a banner emblazoned with the symbol of Excalibur.

Rhys raised his hand in greeting once more. "Welcome, noble knights! We seek the legendary sword Excalibur and the wisdom of the wizards who dwell here."

The lead knight dismounted, removing his helmet to reveal a stern but kind face. "I am Sir Gareth, protector of these lands. You speak of Excalibur and wizards. What is your purpose here?"

Zephyrus stepped forward. "We are travelers from another time, seeking knowledge and understanding. We have heard tales of the great sword Excalibur and the powerful wizards who reside in these lands. We wish to learn from them and offer our assistance in return."

Sir Gareth regarded them with a mix of suspicion and curiosity. "Travelers from another time? Your words are strange, but I sense truth in them. Very well, I will take you to see the wizards. They are not far from here, in a place known as the Enchanted Grove."

As they followed Sir Gareth and his knights, Rhys continued to explain the intricacies of the mushroom cults and their connection to the wizards. "These wizards, through their connection to the ancient fungi, have created a society that blends the mystical and the practical. They are the guardians of knowledge, and their wisdom could be invaluable to us."

Zephyrus nodded, feeling the weight of their journey. "If we can learn from them and bring that knowledge back to our own time, we could use it to further our understanding of the Hyperverse and ensure its balance."

The Enchanted Grove was a place of breathtaking beauty. Ancient trees towered above them, their leaves shimmering with an otherworldly light. The air was thick with the scent of blooming flowers and the earthy aroma of mushrooms. In the center of the grove stood a circle of stone, glowing with a soft, pulsating light.

As they approached, a figure stepped forward from the shadows. He was tall and slender, with a flowing beard and eyes that sparkled with wisdom. "Welcome, travelers," he said, his voice resonant and warm. "I am Merlin, guardian of the Enchanted Grove. What brings you to our sacred place?"

Zephyrus bowed respectfully. "Great Merlin, we seek knowledge and guidance. We come from a time far removed from this one, and we have heard tales of your wisdom and power. We wish to learn from you and to share what we know in return."

Merlin's eyes twinkled with curiosity. "Travelers from another time, seeking wisdom. This is indeed a rare occurrence. Very well, I shall share what I know, but you must also share your knowledge with us. There is much we can learn from each other."

As they sat in the circle of stone, Merlin began to explain the ancient practices of the wizards and their connection to the mystical fungi. "These fungi are the lifeblood of our magic. They connect us to the very essence of the earth, allowing us to perform feats that seem impossible. Through them, we gain wisdom, strength, and the ability to influence the world around us."

Zephyrus and Rhys shared their own knowledge of the Hyperverse, explaining the complexities of time and space, and how beings could exist in multiple realities simultaneously. Merlin listened intently, his eyes gleaming with understanding.

"The Hyperverse," he mused. "A realm of infinite possibilities. This knowledge could indeed be powerful. Perhaps we can use it to strengthen our magic, to ensure the balance of our world and yours."

As they continued to exchange knowledge, Zephyrus felt a profound sense of unity. The past and the future were intertwined, each influencing the other in ways that were both subtle and profound. Through their combined wisdom, they could ensure the balance of the Hyperverse and the harmony of all realities.

With Merlin's guidance, they began to experiment with blending the ancient magic of the fungi with the advanced understanding of the Hyperverse. The results were astounding. They created new forms of magic that could influence time and space, enhancing their ability to navigate the complexities of the Hyperverse.

"Together," Merlin declared, "we can achieve great things. The knowledge of the past and the wisdom of the future, united in purpose. This is the true power of the Hyperverse."

As they stood in the Enchanted Grove, Zephyrus felt a sense of fulfillment. The journey was far from over, but with the combined strength of their allies and the wisdom they had gained, they were ready to face whatever challenges lay ahead. The Hyperverse awaited, a vast expanse of possibilities, and they were ready to explore every corner, uncover every secret, and ensure that the balance was maintained for all eternity.

In the midst of their explorations and exchanges, Zephyrus couldn't help but notice the growing bond between Rhys and Elara. Despite the complexities of their past, Zephyrus felt a sense of peace. He had shared an eternity in an instant with Elara in the Hyperverse nexus within The Elaraeon, and their relationship had evolved into something different but no less significant. He harbored no resentment, understanding that Rhys and Elara's connection was a natural progression of their journey.

As Rhys and Elara grew closer, Zephyrus focused on his role in guiding and protecting the Hyperverse. He knew that their collective efforts were essential to maintaining the delicate balance of all realities. Together, with the wisdom of Merlin and the support of their friends, they would continue their journey, navigating the infinite possibilities of the Hyperverse with courage, compassion, and unity.

Rhys, drenched from the rain, raised his right hand in greeting as he spotted Zephyrus. "Hola, Zephyrus! I'm here in medieval times to greet Excalibur!"

Zephyrus smiled, acknowledging his friend's enthusiasm despite the downpour. "Yes, Morgan learns through inundation about gang activity through Yanni. The portal in her house appeared as Mordriad and led to medieval times. Our best friend ventures through for jousting and chivalrous adventures."

Rhys nodded, excitement gleaming in his eyes. "I've heard that wizards are here, and I've created modern times in our world through a mushroom cult."

Zephyrus chuckled at the audacity of his friend's exploits. "Wizards? And a mushroom cult? Tell me more."

As they walked down the drenched road, Rhys explained the unusual circumstances that had led him to this medieval world. "Morgan, or Mordriad as he's known in this realm, discovered a portal in Yanni's house. This portal is linked to a nexus device that allows us to traverse time and space. Through this, he has learned about the complexities of gang activity in modern times, using this knowledge to influence and create a new reality in the past."

Zephyrus listened intently, the rain soaking through his clothes but his mind alight with curiosity. "So, Mordriad is manipulating the past to shape the future?"

"Exactly," Rhys replied. "But there's more. In this medieval world, wizards wield great power, and their influence is vast. They use a form of magic derived from ancient fungi, a precursor to what we now understand as mushroom cults in our time."

Zephyrus considered this. "So, the wizards here are essentially the ancestors of the mushroom cults we've encountered in modern times?"

"Yes," Rhys confirmed. "They use the mystical properties of these fungi to perform extraordinary feats. Mordriad, through his manipulations, has introduced elements of modernity into this world, creating a blend of magic and technology that is both fascinating and dangerous."

Their conversation was interrupted by the sound of hoofbeats. They turned to see a group of knights approaching, their armor gleaming despite the rain. At their head was a knight carrying a banner emblazoned with the symbol of Excalibur.

Rhys raised his hand in greeting once more. "Welcome, noble knights! We seek the legendary sword Excalibur and the wisdom of the wizards who dwell here."

The lead knight dismounted, removing his helmet to reveal a stern but kind face. "I am Sir Gareth, protector of these lands. You speak of Excalibur and wizards. What is your purpose here?"

Zephyrus stepped forward. "We are travelers from another time, seeking knowledge and understanding. We have heard tales of the great sword Excalibur and the powerful wizards who reside in these lands. We wish to learn from them and offer our assistance in return."

Sir Gareth regarded them with a mix of suspicion and curiosity. "Travelers from another time? Your words are strange, but I sense truth in them. Very well, I will take you to see the wizards. They are not far from here, in a place known as the Enchanted Grove."

As they followed Sir Gareth and his knights, Rhys continued to explain the intricacies of the mushroom cults and their connection to the wizards. "These wizards, through their connection to the ancient fungi, have created a society that blends the mystical and the practical. They are the guardians of knowledge, and their wisdom could be invaluable to us."

Zephyrus nodded, feeling the weight of their journey. "If we can learn from them and bring that knowledge back to our own time, we could use it to further our understanding of the Hyperverse and ensure its balance."

The Enchanted Grove was a place of breathtaking beauty. Ancient trees towered above them, their leaves shimmering with an otherworldly light. The air was thick with the scent of blooming flowers and the earthy aroma of mushrooms. In the center of the grove stood a circle of stone, glowing with a soft, pulsating light.

As they approached, a figure stepped forward from the shadows. He was tall and slender, with a flowing beard and eyes that sparkled with wisdom. "Welcome, travelers," he said, his voice resonant and warm. "I am Merlin, guardian of the Enchanted Grove. What brings you to our sacred place?"

Zephyrus bowed respectfully. "Great Merlin, we seek knowledge and guidance. We come from a time far removed from this one, and we have heard tales of your wisdom and power. We wish to learn from you and to share what we know in return."

Merlin's eyes twinkled with curiosity. "Travelers from another time, seeking wisdom. This is indeed a rare occurrence. Very well, I shall share what I know, but you must also share your knowledge with us. There is much we can learn from each other."

As they sat in the circle of stone, Merlin began to explain the ancient practices of the wizards and their connection to the mystical fungi. "These fungi are the lifeblood of our magic. They connect us to the very essence of the earth, allowing us to perform feats that seem impossible. Through them, we gain wisdom, strength, and the ability to influence the world around us."

Zephyrus and Rhys shared their own knowledge of the Hyperverse, explaining the complexities of time and space, and how beings could exist in multiple realities simultaneously. Merlin listened intently, his eyes gleaming with understanding.

"The Hyperverse," he mused. "A realm of infinite possibilities. This knowledge could indeed be powerful. Perhaps we can use it to strengthen our magic, to ensure the balance of our world and yours."

As they continued to exchange knowledge, Zephyrus felt a profound sense of unity. The past and the future were intertwined, each influencing the other in ways that were both subtle and profound. Through their combined wisdom, they could ensure the balance of the Hyperverse and the harmony of all realities.

With Merlin's guidance, they began to experiment with blending the ancient magic of the fungi with the advanced understanding of the Hyperverse. The results were astounding. They created new forms of magic that could influence time and space, enhancing their ability to navigate the complexities of the Hyperverse.

"Together," Merlin declared, "we can achieve great things. The knowledge of the past and the wisdom of the future, united in purpose. This is the true power of the Hyperverse."

As they stood in the Enchanted Grove, Zephyrus felt a sense of fulfillment. The journey was far from over, but with the combined strength of their allies and the wisdom they had gained, they were ready to face whatever challenges lay ahead. The Hyperverse awaited, a vast expanse of possibilities, and they were ready to explore every corner, uncover every secret, and ensure that the balance was maintained for all eternity.

In the midst of their explorations and exchanges, Zephyrus couldn't help but notice the growing bond between Rhys and Elara. Despite the complexities of their past, Zephyrus felt a sense of peace. He had shared an eternity in an instant with Elara in the Hyperverse nexus within The Elaraeon, and their relationship had evolved into something different but no less significant. He harbored no resentment, understanding that Rhys and Elara's connection was a natural progression of their journey.

As Rhys and Elara grew closer, Zephyrus focused on his role in guiding and protecting the Hyperverse. He knew that their collective efforts were essential to maintaining the delicate balance of all realities. Together, with the wisdom of Merlin and the support of their friends, they would continue their journey, navigating the infinite possibilities of the Hyperverse with courage, compassion, and unity.

Zephyrus walked in silence, the steady patter of rain drumming on his cloak. His thoughts were tangled, a knot of emotions he hadn't entirely unraveled. Rhys had always been his closest confidant, and Elara had once been the love of his life. The intricate dance of their relationships had changed over time, particularly within the infinite possibilities of the Hyperverse.

Breaking the silence, Zephyrus glanced at Rhys. "You know I told you," he began, his voice measured, "how I felt about Elara."

Rhys slowed his pace, turning to look at Zephyrus, his expression a mix of concern and understanding. "I remember," he replied. "You said you were okay with it. That your feelings for her had changed."

Zephyrus sighed, wiping a few stray raindrops from his brow. "I did. And I am. It's just... complicated. We shared so much, so many moments that feel like an eternity. But in the nexus of the Hyperverse, time has a way of shifting perspectives."

Rhys nodded thoughtfully. "I know it's complicated. Elara and I never meant to make things difficult for you. It's just that... being with her feels right."

Zephyrus stopped walking and turned to face Rhys fully. "I'm not upset with you or with her. It's just that seeing you together brings back memories. It's something I have to work through."

Rhys placed a reassuring hand on Zephyrus's shoulder. "We'll get through this together. Our friendship means too much to let anything come between us."

Zephyrus gave a small, appreciative smile. "Thank you, Rhys. I needed to hear that."

As they continued their journey, the rain began to let up, revealing a sky streaked with the soft hues of dawn. They approached the edge of the Enchanted Grove, the ancient trees standing as silent sentinels to the knowledge and power within.

Merlin emerged from the shadows, his presence commanding yet gentle. "Welcome back, travelers. I trust your journey has been enlightening."

Zephyrus nodded. "It has, Merlin. We've learned much, but there's still so much to understand."

The wizard smiled knowingly. "Knowledge is an endless journey, Zephyrus. But you are on the right path. Now, let us delve deeper into the mysteries of the Hyperverse and the ancient magics of this world."

They gathered around a large stone table in the center of the grove, its surface etched with intricate runes that seemed to glow faintly in the dim light. Merlin spread out several ancient scrolls and began to explain the complex interconnections between the magical fungi of the past and the advanced technologies of the Hyperverse.

"These fungi," Merlin said, pointing to an illustration of a luminescent mushroom, "are the key to our power. They connect us to the earth, to the energy that flows through all living things. In your time, these connections have evolved into what you call the Hyperverse."

Zephyrus listened intently, absorbing every detail. "So, the Hyperverse is like an advanced form of this ancient magic?"

"Precisely," Merlin replied. "The Hyperverse allows you to manipulate time and space, much like our magic does. But with your knowledge, we can take this a step further. We can create a synthesis of magic and technology that will enhance our abilities and expand our understanding."

Rhys leaned in, fascinated. "And how do we achieve this synthesis?"

Merlin's eyes sparkled with excitement. "By combining the essence of the fungi with the principles of the Hyperverse. We must conduct a series of experiments to see how these elements interact."

As they worked, Zephyrus couldn't help but notice the subtle glances exchanged between Rhys and Elara. Despite his efforts to remain detached, a pang of jealousy flared within him. He pushed it aside, focusing instead on the task at hand.

They spent hours blending the ancient magics with Hyperverse principles, creating new spells and devices that seemed to bridge the gap between their worlds. One such creation was a crystalline orb infused with the essence of the fungi, designed to enhance one's connection to the Hyperverse.

"This orb," Merlin explained, holding it up for them to see, "will allow you to navigate the Hyperverse with greater precision. It will amplify your abilities and help you maintain balance within the realms."

Zephyrus took the orb, feeling its power resonate through him. "This is incredible. Thank you, Merlin."

The wizard nodded. "It is only the beginning. There is much more to discover."

As the day turned to night, they sat around a fire, the warmth and light providing a welcome respite from the chill of the evening. Rhys and Elara sat close together, their whispered conversations and shared smiles a stark reminder of their growing bond.

Zephyrus, feeling a mixture of contentment and melancholy, decided to take a walk to clear his mind. The Enchanted Grove was beautiful at night, the bioluminescent fungi casting a soft, ethereal glow on everything they touched.

As he wandered through the grove, he heard footsteps behind him. Turning, he saw Elara approaching, her expression gentle but concerned.

"Zephyrus," she said softly, "can we talk?"

He nodded, gesturing for her to join him. They walked in silence for a few moments before she spoke again.

"I know this isn't easy for you," she began. "Seeing Rhys and me together. I never wanted to hurt you."

Zephyrus sighed, stopping to look at her. "I know, Elara. It's just... a lot to process. But I care about both of you, and I want you to be happy."

She smiled, a hint of sadness in her eyes. "You've always been so understanding. I just want you to know that we're here for you, no matter what."

He returned her smile, feeling a weight lift from his shoulders. "Thank you, Elara. That means a lot to me."

They continued their walk, talking about their past adventures and the journey ahead. By the time they returned to the camp, Zephyrus felt a sense of peace he hadn't felt in a long time.

The next morning, they resumed their work with Merlin, eager to continue their experiments and learn more about the interplay between ancient magic and Hyperverse technology. Zephyrus focused intently on their tasks, finding solace in the complexities of their work.

Merlin observed their progress with a keen eye, occasionally offering guidance or insights. "You are making remarkable strides," he remarked one afternoon. "Your understanding of the Hyperverse and its potential is truly impressive."

Zephyrus felt a swell of pride at the compliment. "Thank you, Merlin. Your teachings have been invaluable."

As days turned into weeks, the bonds between them grew stronger, their shared purpose creating a sense of camaraderie and mutual respect. Despite the lingering feelings of jealousy, Zephyrus found himself increasingly at ease with Rhys and Elara's relationship, recognizing that their happiness did not diminish his own.

One evening, as they sat around the fire, Rhys turned to Zephyrus, a thoughtful expression on his face. "Zephyrus, I've been thinking about our next steps. There's still so much to learn, and we've made incredible progress here. But what if we took this knowledge back to our time? What if we used it to influence the Hyperverse in new ways?"

Zephyrus considered the idea, nodding slowly. "It's a bold plan, Rhys. But it could be exactly what we need to ensure the balance of the Hyperverse."

Merlin smiled, a twinkle in his eye. "You are ready. The knowledge you've gained here will serve you well in your time. Remember, the journey is never truly over. There will always be more to discover, more to learn."

With Merlin's blessing, they prepared to return to their own time, taking with them the new spells and devices they had created. The journey back through the Hyperverse was a familiar one, the shifting landscapes and swirling energies a testament to the infinite possibilities that awaited them.

As they stepped back into their own world, Zephyrus felt a renewed sense of purpose. He looked at Rhys and Elara, their faces filled with determination and hope. Together, they would continue their journey, using the knowledge they had gained to navigate the complexities of the Hyperverse and ensure its balance.

Their adventures were far from over, and Zephyrus knew that challenges awaited them. But with the strength of their friendship and the wisdom they had gained, they were ready to face whatever came their way. The Hyperverse was vast and ever-changing, but they were united in their purpose, bound by the intricate web of existence that defined their reality.

As they moved forward, Zephyrus felt a deep sense of gratitude for the experiences they had shared and the bonds they had formed. The path ahead was uncertain, but he was confident that together, they could navigate the infinite possibilities of the Hyperverse with courage, compassion, and unity.

The journey continued, a cycle of discovery, understanding, and growth. And as Zephyrus embraced the future, he knew that he was never alone. He was all that he had been and all that he would become, navigating the infinite possibilities of the Hyperverse with the support of his friends and the wisdom of the ages.

Zephyrus stood on the threshold of the Hyperverse, his mind abuzz with the possibilities that lay ahead. The knowledge they had acquired from Merlin and the ancient wizards had opened new doors, blending the mystical with the technological in ways they had never imagined. The journey back through the Hyperverse had been enlightening, but the real challenges awaited them in their own time.

The mushrooms and vapors they had learned about worked in fascinating ways, deeply tied to the disinhibitor hypothesis. These substances were not merely tools for altered states; they were gateways to expanded consciousness and heightened awareness, allowing those who used them to access realms of experience that were otherwise inaccessible. Zephyrus was acutely aware of the potential these substances held, but also the dangers they posed if not used wisely.

One evening, as they sat around a campfire, the glow casting dancing shadows on their faces, Rhys leaned forward, his eyes reflecting the flickering flames. "Zephyrus, these mushrooms and vapors we've encountered—they do more than just alter perception, don't they? They seem to open doors to other realities."

Zephyrus nodded, contemplating the intricate mechanisms at play. "Yes, Rhys. They work along the lines of the disinhibitor hypothesis. By lowering the barriers of the mind, they allow users to access parts of the brain that are usually dormant. This can result in voices and visions that seem incredibly real, even if they stem from realms of unknown experience."

Elara, sitting beside Rhys, added, "The experiences I've had with them have been profound. It's as if they connect me to something greater, something beyond our usual understanding of reality. But we must be careful. These substances can be powerful allies, but also dangerous if misused."

Zephyrus agreed. "The voices and visions of XOXO and Baby Morgan are believable because they come from a place of expanded consciousness. When our awareness is heightened, we tap into the Hyperverse more directly. But we need to understand and respect the limits of this expanded state."

Old XOXO, ever present in their minds, chose this moment to speak. "Zephyrus, Rhys, Elara," the voice began, soothing yet commanding. "You must learn to navigate these expanded states with caution. Let me show you the path."

A soft light enveloped them, and suddenly they found themselves in a dreamlike landscape, vibrant and surreal. It was as if they had been transported to a place where the boundaries of reality were fluid, where the mind could explore without the constraints of the physical world.

XOXO's presence was stronger here, almost tangible. "This is the realm of heightened awareness," XOXO explained. "Here, the disinhibitor hypothesis plays out in full. The barriers between your conscious and subconscious minds are lowered, allowing you to access deeper truths and greater wisdom."

Zephyrus felt a rush of understanding. "So, this is how the mushrooms and vapors work. They bring us to this state where we can experience the Hyperverse more directly."

"Exactly," XOXO confirmed. "But with great power comes great responsibility. You must learn to control these experiences, to guide them rather than be overwhelmed by them."

The landscape around them shifted, showing scenes from their past and possible futures. Zephyrus saw himself as a child, playing with Baby Morgan, the innocence of their early years stark against the backdrop of their current struggles. He saw Rhys and Elara, their bond growing stronger, and felt a pang of bittersweet acceptance.

Elara reached out, touching a vision of her younger self. "These experiences... they are so real. It's like reliving my memories and dreams."

Rhys, standing beside her, watched a scene of his own past, his eyes softening with nostalgia. "It's incredible. We can see our lives from different perspectives, understand our choices and their consequences."

XOXO's voice guided them further. "This is the essence of the Hyperverse. Every choice, every action creates ripples across time and space. By understanding these ripples, you can navigate your path with greater wisdom."

As they continued their journey through the dreamscape, Old XOXO began to teach them techniques for harnessing the power of the disinhibitor hypothesis. "First, you must learn to ground yourselves," XOXO instructed. "Find a point of focus, something that anchors you to your reality."

Zephyrus closed his eyes, focusing on the warmth of the campfire, the sound of the crackling wood. He felt a sense of stability, a connection to the present moment that allowed him to navigate the shifting landscape of his mind.

"Good," XOXO praised. "Now, let your mind wander, but maintain your focus. Allow the visions to come, but do not lose yourself in them."

As Zephyrus followed XOXO's guidance, he began to see visions of possible futures. He saw himself leading a group of explorers through the Hyperverse, their journey filled with discovery and wonder. He saw Rhys and Elara by his side, their bond unbreakable, their love a source of strength.

Elara, guided by XOXO, saw her own path intertwining with Zephyrus's. She saw herself becoming a leader, using her knowledge of the Hyperverse to guide others. She saw the challenges they would face, but also the triumphs, the moments of connection and understanding that made the journey worthwhile.

Rhys, too, saw his future. He saw himself as a protector, using his strength and wisdom to safeguard those he cared about. He saw his relationship with Elara growing deeper, their love a beacon of hope in the ever-changing landscape of the Hyperverse.

XOXO's voice brought them back to the present. "These visions are not set in stone. They are possibilities, potential paths that you can choose to follow or change. The power of the Hyperverse lies in its infinite possibilities, and you have the ability to shape your own destiny."

Zephyrus opened his eyes, the dreamscape fading as he returned to the reality of the campfire. "Thank you, XOXO. We have much to learn, but I feel more prepared now."

Rhys and Elara nodded in agreement, their faces reflecting the same sense of understanding and determination.

"We will use this knowledge wisely," Rhys said, his voice firm. "We will navigate the Hyperverse with caution and respect, using our experiences to guide us."

Elara added, "We will honor the power of the mushrooms and vapors, recognizing their ability to expand our consciousness and connect us to the greater whole. But we will also remember the importance of grounding ourselves, of maintaining our connection to reality."

XOXO's voice was filled with approval. "You have learned well. Continue on your journey with this wisdom, and you will find the balance you seek."

As the night wore on, they shared their visions and experiences, discussing the lessons they had learned and the paths they might take. Zephyrus felt a renewed sense of purpose, a clarity that had been lacking before. The Hyperverse was a vast and complex realm, but with the guidance of XOXO and the support of his friends, he felt ready to face whatever challenges lay ahead.

The next morning, they began to implement the techniques they had learned. They experimented with the mushrooms and vapors, carefully navigating the expanded states of consciousness they induced. They practiced grounding themselves, using their points of focus to maintain stability even as their minds explored the far reaches of the Hyperverse.

Zephyrus found that his understanding of the Hyperverse deepened with each experience. He could see the connections between events, the ripples that spread across time and space. He learned to anticipate the consequences of his actions, to guide his path with greater wisdom.

Rhys and Elara, too, found their abilities growing stronger. Rhys became more attuned to the protective aspects of the Hyperverse, using his strength and resilience to safeguard their journey. Elara's leadership qualities shone through, her ability to navigate the complexities of the Hyperverse guiding their group with confidence and compassion.

Together, they faced new challenges, each one a test of their newfound skills and understanding. They encountered beings from other realities, entities who sought to disrupt the balance of the Hyperverse. But with their combined strength and the knowledge they had gained, they were able to navigate these challenges, maintaining the harmony they sought.

One particularly intense experience involved a confrontation with a being known as the Temporal Wraith, a shadowy figure who fed on the dissonance of time. The Wraith had been disrupting the flow of the Hyperverse, creating chaos and instability.

Zephyrus, Rhys, and Elara prepared for the encounter, using the techniques XOXO had taught them. As they faced the Wraith, they focused on grounding themselves, maintaining their connection to reality even as they navigated the expanded states of consciousness.

The battle was fierce, the Wraith's attacks sending ripples of dissonance through the Hyperverse. But Zephyrus and his friends held their ground, using their connection to the Hyperverse to counter the Wraith's influence. They channeled the power of the mushrooms and vapors, their heightened awareness allowing them to anticipate the Wraith's movements and counter its attacks.

In a final, climactic moment, Zephyrus used the crystalline orb they had created with Merlin's guidance. The orb's power amplified their connection to the Hyperverse, creating a surge of energy that overwhelmed the Wraith. With a final, piercing shriek, the Wraith was banished, its presence dissipating into the ether.

As the echoes of the battle faded, Zephyrus, Rhys, and Elara stood together, their bond stronger than ever. They had faced a formidable foe and emerged victorious, their understanding of the Hyperverse deepened by the experience.

"We did it," Rhys said, his voice filled with pride.

As Zephyrus, Rhys, and Elara continued their journey, their thoughts frequently turned to the powerful deity known as Mordriad. He was not just a figure of myth or legend but a tangible presence within the Hyperverse. Mordriad existed in a temporal continuum, perpetually hovering in an orbit around Io, one of Jupiter's moons. His existence was bound to a celestial event reminiscent of the Big Crunch, a cataclysmic event that would eventually lead to the universe's collapse and subsequent rebirth. This cyclical destruction and creation formed the core of Mordriad's power and purpose.

Mordriad's presence was both awe-inspiring and daunting. He was a god whose influence stretched across time and space, a being who could manipulate the very fabric of reality. The trio knew that approaching Mordriad required a special nexus device, an artifact capable of opening portals not only through time and space but also to Mordriad's hover above Io.

One evening, as they gathered around their campfire, Zephyrus shared his concerns. "We need to understand more about Mordriad before we can approach him. His power is immense, and his intentions are beyond our comprehension."

Rhys nodded, his expression thoughtful. "From what we've learned, Mordriad is deeply connected to the cycles of the universe. His existence tied to the Big Crunch means he's a guardian of sorts, ensuring the balance between destruction and rebirth."

Elara, ever the strategist, added, "We should start by understanding the nexus device. If we can figure out how to use it, we might be able to gain insight into Mordriad's motives and perhaps communicate with him."

They spent the next several days studying the nexus device. It was a beautifully intricate piece of technology, a sphere etched with runes and glowing with an inner light. The device seemed almost alive, responding to their touch and resonating with the energies of the Hyperverse.

Zephyrus held the nexus device in his hands, feeling its power pulse through him. "This device is more than just a portal. It's a conduit for Mordriad's influence. It can connect us directly to him, but we need to be careful. We don't know what kind of impact this could have on us or the Hyperverse."

Rhys leaned closer, examining the device. "We should test it in a controlled manner. Open a small portal, observe the effects, and then decide our next steps."

They chose a secluded spot in the forest, away from any disturbances. With Rhys and Elara standing by, Zephyrus activated the nexus device. The runes on its surface glowed brighter, and a swirling vortex of light appeared before them. The portal shimmered, its edges flickering with energy.

Through the portal, they could see Io, its surface a chaotic landscape of volcanic activity. In the distance, they spotted Mordriad's hover, a sleek and otherworldly structure that defied the natural laws of physics. It floated effortlessly above Io, radiating an aura of immense power.

Elara gasped, her eyes wide with wonder. "There it is. Mordriad's hover."

Zephyrus nodded, his gaze fixed on the structure. "We need to proceed with caution. Let's start by sending a probe through the portal to gather data."

They had prepared a small, autonomous drone equipped with sensors and cameras. Zephyrus guided the drone through the portal, watching as it crossed the threshold and began transmitting data back to them.

The images and readings were astonishing. The hover was a marvel of advanced technology, seamlessly blending organic and inorganic components. The energy readings indicated that it was drawing power directly from Io's volcanic activity and the surrounding space.

As the drone approached the hover, they received a sudden spike in the data. The readings became erratic, and the images distorted. Then, the transmission cut off entirely.

Rhys frowned, checking the equipment. "We've lost the signal. It seems that Mordriad's hover has some sort of defense mechanism."

Zephyrus deactivated the portal, the vortex closing with a soft hiss. "We'll need to find a way to counteract those defenses if we want to make contact."

They spent the next few days analyzing the data they had collected, looking for any patterns or weaknesses in Mordriad's defenses. During this time, Zephyrus couldn't shake the feeling that they were being watched, as if Mordriad was aware of their efforts and was subtly guiding them.

One night, as they pored over the data, Zephyrus heard a faint whisper in his mind. It was XOXO, the presence that had guided him through so many challenges. "Zephyrus," XOXO said, "Mordriad knows you are seeking him. He is curious, but he is also wary. You must show him that you mean no harm."

Zephyrus relayed this to Rhys and Elara. "We need to find a way to communicate our intentions to Mordriad. If we can show him that we seek knowledge and understanding, not power, he might be more receptive."

Elara suggested, "Perhaps we can use the nexus device to send a message. Something simple but honest."

They crafted a message, explaining who they were, their journey through the Hyperverse, and their desire to learn from Mordriad. Zephyrus activated the nexus device once more, opening a small portal and sending the message through.

For a while, there was silence. Then, the portal shimmered, and a voice echoed through their minds. It was deep and resonant, filled with an ancient wisdom that seemed to vibrate through the very air around them.

"Travelers of the Hyperverse," the voice said, "I am Mordriad. Your quest for knowledge has not gone unnoticed. I have seen your efforts and understand your intentions. Approach with the nexus device, and we shall meet."

Zephyrus felt a mixture of relief and trepidation. "Mordriad has acknowledged us. He has invited us to approach."

Rhys smiled, a sense of accomplishment evident on his face. "This is our chance to learn from a being who spans time and space. Let's not waste it."

With the portal fully opened, they stepped through, feeling the familiar pull of the Hyperverse as they crossed the threshold. The landscape of Io greeted them, its volatile surface a stark contrast to the serene beauty of the Enchanted Grove.

Mordriad's hover loomed above them, a beacon of power and knowledge. As they approached, a section of the hover opened, revealing an entryway bathed in soft, welcoming light.

Inside, they found themselves in a vast chamber filled with intricate machinery and glowing runes. At the center of the chamber stood Mordriad, his form both human and otherworldly. He radiated an aura of calm authority, his eyes reflecting the depths of the universe.

"Welcome, Zephyrus, Rhys, Elara," Mordriad said, his voice resonating through the chamber. "You have come far and faced many challenges. What do you seek from me?"

Zephyrus stepped forward, his voice steady. "We seek knowledge and understanding. We wish to learn about the cycles of the universe, the balance between destruction and rebirth, and how we can help maintain that balance within the Hyperverse."

Mordriad nodded, his expression thoughtful. "Your quest is noble. The cycles of the universe are indeed complex, but they are essential for maintaining the balance. Destruction and rebirth are two sides of the same coin, each necessary for the continuation of existence."

Elara asked, "How do you control these cycles? How do you ensure that the balance is maintained?"

Mordriad gestured to the machinery around them. "This hover and the nexus device are my tools. They allow me to manipulate time and space, to influence the flow of events. But it is not just about control. It is about understanding the natural order and working within it."

Rhys looked around, awe in his eyes. "And what about the animals on Earth? We've heard that you are learning to control them for tampering and manipulation in time."

Mordriad smiled, a hint of amusement in his expression. "Indeed, the creatures of Earth are part of the tapestry of life. By understanding their behaviors and patterns, I can subtly influence events, guiding them toward a balanced outcome. It is a delicate process, one that requires patience and precision."

Zephyrus felt a deep sense of respect for Mordriad's role. "We want to help. We have learned much from our journey, and we believe we can contribute to maintaining the balance."

Mordriad regarded them with a measured gaze. "Your willingness to learn and to help is commendable. There is much you can do, but you must always remember the importance of balance. Power without wisdom leads to chaos."

They spent the next several hours in deep discussion, learning from Mordriad's vast knowledge and sharing their own experiences. Mordriad showed them how to use the nexus device more effectively, teaching them techniques for navigating the Hyperverse and influencing the cycles of time and space.

As they prepared to leave, Mordriad gave them a final piece of advice. "Remember, the Hyperverse is a place of infinite possibilities. It is your actions and choices that shape its course. Use the knowledge you have gained wisely, and always strive for balance."

With a renewed sense of purpose, Zephyrus, Rhys, and Elara returned to their own time. The journey had deepened their understanding of the Hyperverse and their role within it. They knew that the path ahead would be filled with challenges, but with the guidance of Mordriad and the wisdom they had gained, they felt ready to face whatever came next.

As they stepped back through the portal, the familiar landscape of their world greeted them. The Hyperverse awaited, a vast expanse of possibilities, and they were ready to explore every corner, uncover every secret, and ensure that the balance was maintained for all eternity.

Zephyrus, Rhys, and Elara had barely returned from their meeting with Mordriad when they were confronted with yet another enigma of the Hyperverse. The journey had only intensified their thirst for knowledge, and it seemed the Hyperverse was eager to oblige. This time, their focus turned to an ancient and mysterious crystal entity known for its ability to compute fortunes using magnetic resonance.

As they gathered around their campfire, Zephyrus shared what little he knew about the entity. "I've heard tales of a crystal being that resides deep within the Hyperverse. It's said to use magnetic resonance to calculate and predict fortunes. Some believe it can see the threads of destiny more clearly than any other."

Rhys, his curiosity piqued, leaned forward. "Magnetic resonance? Like the way we use magnets to interact with electronic fields?"

"Exactly," Zephyrus confirmed. "But on a far more sophisticated level. The entity uses the natural magnetic fields of the Hyperverse to compute and understand the complex web of destinies."

Elara, always the strategist, looked thoughtful. "If we can find this crystal entity, we might gain insights into our own paths and the larger balance of the Hyperverse. It could be invaluable."

Their decision made, the trio set off, guided by the faint, pulsating energy they could feel at the edges of their perception. The Hyperverse, with its ever-shifting landscapes and realities, required them to be constantly vigilant, but also allowed them to exist in multiple places at once. This peculiar trait of the Hyperverse meant they could cover vast distances and explore multiple avenues simultaneously.

As they journeyed deeper, the environment around them began to change. The air became charged with a subtle, humming energy, and the ground beneath their feet seemed to pulse with a life of its own. They knew they were getting closer.

Suddenly, the landscape shifted dramatically. They found themselves in a vast cavern, its walls glittering with countless crystals that reflected the ambient light in mesmerizing patterns. In the center of the cavern stood a massive crystal structure, its form both geometric and organic, pulsating with a radiant blue light.

Rhys took a cautious step forward. "This must be it. The crystal entity."

As they approached, the light from the crystal intensified, and a voice echoed through the cavern, clear and resonant. "Welcome, travelers of the Hyperverse. I am the Crystal Oracle, keeper of fortunes and destinies. What brings you to my domain?"

Zephyrus stepped forward, his voice steady but filled with reverence. "Great Oracle, we seek knowledge and guidance. We wish to understand our paths within the Hyperverse and ensure the balance of all realities."

The Crystal Oracle's light pulsed rhythmically, as if considering their request. "You seek to understand the threads of destiny. Very well. I will compute your fortunes using the magnetic resonance that binds this realm. Step forward, and let the resonance reveal your paths."

As they each stepped closer, they felt a gentle vibration envelop them, the magnetic fields interacting with their very beings. The sensation was both soothing and invigorating, as if they were being attuned to the frequencies of the Hyperverse itself.

Rhys was the first to speak. "What do you see for me, Oracle?"

The Crystal Oracle's light intensified, and an image formed within its crystalline depths. "Rhys, protector of the paths, your destiny is to safeguard the balance. You will face trials that test your strength and resolve, but your courage will light the way for others."

Rhys nodded, feeling the truth of the Oracle's words resonate within him. "I will do my best to fulfill this destiny."

Next, Elara stepped forward. "What of me, Oracle?"

The light shifted, revealing another vision. "Elara, guide of the lost, your wisdom and compassion will be a beacon for those who wander. You will uncover secrets long hidden and lead others to understanding and unity."

Elara felt a deep sense of purpose. "Thank you, Oracle. I will strive to be the guide you describe."

Finally, Zephyrus approached. "And what is my fortune, Oracle?"

The Crystal Oracle's light grew even brighter, filling the cavern with a dazzling glow. "Zephyrus, seeker of truths, your path is one of discovery and revelation. You will uncover the deepest mysteries of the Hyperverse and use this knowledge to maintain the balance. But be wary, for with great knowledge comes great responsibility."

Zephyrus absorbed the Oracle's words, understanding the weight of his journey. "I accept this responsibility. Thank you, Oracle."

The Crystal Oracle's light dimmed slightly, signaling the end of the readings. "Go forth, travelers, with the knowledge of your destinies. The Hyperverse is vast, and its balance delicate. Use what you have learned wisely."

As they exited the cavern, the trio felt a renewed sense of purpose. The Crystal Oracle's insights had given them clarity and direction, reinforcing their commitment to their journey.

As they traveled further, they found themselves navigating a region of the Hyperverse where time seemed to flow differently. Moments stretched and contracted, making their journey feel both fleeting and eternal. It was here that they encountered beings from other realms, each with their own stories and destinies intertwined with the fabric of the Hyperverse.

One such being was a wanderer named Thalor, a figure shrouded in mystery. He approached them with a knowing smile, his eyes reflecting the depths of countless experiences. "You are the travelers who spoke with the Crystal Oracle," he said, his voice a melodic blend of curiosity and wisdom.

Zephyrus nodded. "Yes, we are. How do you know of the Oracle?"

Thalor chuckled softly. "The Oracle's influence stretches far and wide. Those who seek knowledge and understanding often find themselves drawn to its light. I, too, have sought the Oracle's guidance."

Elara, ever the diplomat, extended a hand in greeting. "I am Elara, and these are my companions, Rhys and Zephyrus. What brings you to this part of the Hyperverse?"

Thalor accepted her hand with a respectful nod. "I am Thalor, a traveler like yourselves. My journey has taken me across many realms, and I have seen the beauty and chaos that the Hyperverse holds. I am here to offer my assistance, if you would have it."

Rhys, sensing Thalor's sincerity, asked, "What do you seek, Thalor? And how can you help us?"

Thalor's gaze grew distant, as if recalling a memory. "I seek balance, as do you. The Hyperverse is a delicate tapestry, and even the smallest disruption can have far-reaching consequences. I have knowledge of certain paths and connections that may aid you in your quest."

Zephyrus felt a kinship with Thalor, recognizing a kindred spirit. "We welcome your help, Thalor. The more we understand about the Hyperverse, the better we can navigate its complexities."

With Thalor's guidance, they ventured into regions of the Hyperverse that were previously unknown to them. They encountered phenomena that defied conventional understanding—rivers of light that flowed backward in time, mountains that whispered secrets of forgotten worlds, and forests where each leaf held a fragment of a dream.

In one such forest, they discovered a clearing where the air was filled with a soothing hum, a resonance that seemed to connect directly with their minds. Thalor explained, "This is a place of convergence, where multiple realities intersect. It is a rare and powerful location, one that can amplify your connection to the Hyperverse."

Elara closed her eyes, feeling the hum resonate through her. "It's like the entire Hyperverse is singing to us."

Rhys, standing beside her, nodded in agreement. "This place... it feels alive, like it's part of something greater."

Zephyrus, sensing the potential of the clearing, suggested, "We should meditate here, attune ourselves to the resonance. It might help us understand the deeper connections within the Hyperverse."

They sat in the clearing, the hum enveloping them in a cocoon of sound and light. As they meditated, visions began to form in their minds—glimpses of past, present, and future interwoven in a seamless tapestry. They saw the Crystal Oracle, its light guiding countless travelers. They saw Mordriad, hovering above

Io, his influence shaping the flow of time. They saw themselves, their paths intertwining with those of others, each step a part of the grand design.

Thalor's voice, gentle and steady, guided them through the visions. "Remember what you have learned. Each connection, each choice, is part of the balance. Trust in your journey, and you will find your way."

As they emerged from their meditation, they felt a renewed sense of clarity and purpose. The resonance of the clearing had deepened their understanding of the Hyperverse and their role within it.

Zephyrus looked at his companions, his heart filled with gratitude. "Thank you, Thalor. Your guidance has been invaluable."

Thalor smiled, a hint of sadness in his eyes. "My journey continues, as does yours. Remember the lessons you have learned, and may your paths be filled with light."

With Thalor's departure, they resumed their journey, each step guided by the knowledge and insights they had gained. The Hyperverse, with its infinite possibilities, awaited them, and they were ready to face whatever challenges lay ahead.

Their next destination took them to a realm where the very fabric of reality seemed to shimmer with potential. It was a place known as the Nexus of Echoes, where the past and future converged in a perpetual dance. Here, they hoped to gain further insights into their destinies and the balance of the Hyperverse.

As they approached the Nexus, they were greeted by a figure who seemed to exist in multiple times at once.

As they approached the Nexus of Echoes, a shimmering portal where past and future converged, they noticed a figure standing at the entrance. This figure seemed to flicker in and out of existence, as if existing in multiple times at once. Its form was both there and not there, a ghostly presence that defied the usual rules of reality.

Elara, feeling a pull from the Hyperverse, had just departed to attend to a separate task that required her unique skills. Zephyrus and Rhys, left to face the enigmatic figure alone, exchanged a glance filled with both curiosity and caution.

The figure turned towards them, its face a blend of features that seemed to shift with each passing moment. "Welcome, travelers of the Hyperverse," it said, its voice a harmonious blend of past and future tones. "I am the Keeper of the Nexus, a guide to those who seek understanding in this place of convergence."

Zephyrus stepped forward, his gaze steady. "I am Zephyrus, and this is Rhys. We seek knowledge and understanding of our paths within the Hyperverse. Can you help us?"

The Keeper's form flickered, and for a moment, it seemed to split into multiple versions of itself before reuniting. "Indeed, I can assist you. But first, allow me to share a story, one that may illuminate the nature of this place and your own journey."

The Keeper began to weave a tale, its voice creating a tapestry of words that seemed to resonate with the very fabric of the Nexus. "Long ago, when the Hyperverse was young, there existed a race of beings known as the Celestials. These beings were masters of time and space, their wisdom and power unparalleled. They created the Nexus of Echoes as a sanctuary, a place where they could observe and influence the threads of destiny without interfering directly."

Rhys listened intently, his mind absorbing the Keeper's words. "And what became of the Celestials?" he asked.

The Keeper's form shimmered with a hint of melancholy. "The Celestials, in their infinite wisdom, chose to transcend their physical forms, becoming part of the very essence of the Hyperverse. They left behind the Nexus as a gift, a tool for future travelers to use in their quest for balance and understanding."

Zephyrus felt a connection to the story, sensing its deeper truths. "This place, then, is a link to the past and future, a way for us to see and understand the cycles of the Hyperverse more clearly."

"Precisely," the Keeper replied. "But the Nexus is also a test. It reveals truths and possibilities, but it does not dictate your path. You must navigate the threads of destiny with wisdom and care."

As the Keeper spoke, Zephyrus couldn't help but wonder if this enigmatic figure was real. It was rumored that in the Hyperverse, you could never be sure. The Keeper might be a virtual construct, a sophisticated AI created by the Celestials, or even an alien entity masquerading as a guide to socialize humans within the Hyperverse.

"Keeper," Zephyrus began, his tone cautious, "are you real? Or are you a construct of this place, a part of the Hyperverse itself?"

The Keeper's form flickered, a smile playing across its shifting features. "Ah, the nature of reality in the Hyperverse. I am as real as you perceive me to be. My existence is both a reflection of your needs and a creation of the Nexus. Whether I am a virtual construct, an alien, or a remnant of the Celestials, matters less than the wisdom I can offer."

Rhys nodded, understanding the deeper implication. "It's the knowledge and guidance that are important, not the exact nature of the source."

"Exactly," the Keeper agreed. "Now, allow me to show you the threads of your destinies."

The Keeper gestured, and the space around them transformed. They found themselves standing in a vast, ethereal landscape filled with glowing threads of light, each one representing a different path or possibility within the Hyperverse.

Zephyrus felt a sense of awe. "These are our destinies?"

"These are the potential paths you might take," the Keeper clarified. "Each thread is a choice, a decision that will shape your future and the balance of the Hyperverse."

Rhys reached out to touch one of the threads, feeling a surge of energy as it responded to his touch. "This is incredible. Each thread feels alive, like it's part of something greater."

"That is the essence of the Hyperverse," the Keeper explained. "Every action, every choice, creates ripples that affect the whole. Your task is to navigate these threads with wisdom, to choose the paths that will maintain balance and harmony."

Zephyrus focused on the threads before him, sensing the potential within each one. He saw paths where he and his friends faced great challenges, but also achieved remarkable triumphs. He saw moments of profound understanding and deep connections, as well as instances of conflict and struggle.

"The future is not set in stone," the Keeper continued. "It is shaped by your actions and choices. Use the knowledge you have gained to guide your steps, and trust in your ability to find the right path."

Zephyrus and Rhys spent hours exploring the threads of their destinies, guided by the Keeper's wisdom. They saw visions of their future selves, leading others through the complexities of the Hyperverse, uncovering ancient secrets, and ensuring the balance of all realities.

As they delved deeper, they encountered a particularly intriguing thread, one that seemed to glow more brightly than the others. It depicted a future where they discovered a hidden realm within the Hyperverse, a place of unparalleled beauty and knowledge. This realm, known as the Garden of Echoes, was said to hold the key to understanding the deepest mysteries of the Hyperverse.

"Keeper," Zephyrus asked, "what is this Garden of Echoes?"

The Keeper's light pulsed with a sense of reverence. "The Garden of Echoes is a sacred place, a hidden realm where the most profound truths of the Hyperverse are revealed. It is a place of great beauty and wisdom, but also of great challenge. Only those who are truly ready can enter and understand its secrets."

Rhys looked at Zephyrus, excitement and determination in his eyes. "We should find this place. If it holds the key to understanding the Hyperverse, it's worth the journey."

Zephyrus agreed. "But we must be prepared. The challenges we face in the Garden of Echoes will test us like never before."

The Keeper nodded. "You are right to be cautious. The Garden of Echoes is a place of great power, but also great peril. Prepare yourselves well, and trust in the knowledge you have gained."

With the Keeper's guidance, Zephyrus and Rhys began their preparations. They gathered the tools and knowledge they would need for the journey, honing their skills and deepening their understanding of the Hyperverse.

As they worked, Zephyrus couldn't help but think about Elara. She had been called away on her own quest, but he knew she would return when the time was right. Her wisdom and strength would be invaluable in the challenges to come.

Finally, the day came when they were ready to set out for the Garden of Echoes. The Keeper stood before them, its form shimmering with approval. "You have prepared well. The journey ahead will be difficult, but I believe you have the strength and wisdom to succeed."

Zephyrus bowed in gratitude. "Thank you, Keeper. Your guidance has been invaluable."

Rhys added, "We won't let you down. We'll find the Garden of Echoes and uncover its secrets."

With a final nod, the Keeper opened a portal to the Garden of Echoes. The portal shimmered with a radiant light, inviting them to step through.

As they crossed the threshold, they were greeted by a landscape of breathtaking beauty. The Garden of Echoes was a realm of lush greenery, vibrant flowers, and crystalline streams that sparkled in the sunlight. The air was filled with the scent of blooming flowers and the gentle hum of the Hyperverse's resonance.

Zephyrus and Rhys stood in awe, taking in the beauty of the garden. "This place... it's like a paradise," Rhys said, his voice filled with wonder.

Zephyrus nodded, feeling a deep sense of peace and purpose. "But we must remember why we're here. The Garden of Echoes holds the key to understanding the Hyperverse. We need to find that key."

As they ventured deeper into the garden, they encountered beings of light and shadow, guardians of the garden who tested their resolve and wisdom. Each challenge they faced was a lesson, a step towards greater understanding.

In one such encounter, they met a guardian who appeared as a woman of radiant light. Her eyes shone with ancient wisdom, and her voice was like the music of the stars. "Travelers, you have entered the Garden of Echoes seeking knowledge. But knowledge comes with a price. Are you willing to pay it?"

Zephyrus stepped forward, his voice steady. "We are. We seek to understand the Hyperverse and maintain its balance. We will do whatever it takes."

The guardian nodded, her light intensifying. "Very well. To gain the knowledge you seek, you must pass the trials of the garden. Each trial will test a different aspect of your being—your courage, your wisdom, your compassion. Only by succeeding in all the trials will you unlock the secrets of the garden."

With determination in their hearts, Zephyrus and Rhys faced the trials of the Garden of Echoes. Each trial was a journey in itself, a test of their deepest strengths and vulnerabilities.

In one trial, they had to navigate a labyrinth of mirrors, each reflection showing a different aspect of themselves. They had to confront their fears and insecurities, finding their own self for sure this time.

Zephyrus stood on the threshold of the Hyperverse, the shimmering energies around him a constant reminder of the vast possibilities within this realm. His mind was a whirlwind of thoughts, primarily centered on the enigmatic presence of XOXO. Their communication had always been a blend of clarity and confusion, a paradox that reflected the very nature of the Hyperverse.

XOXO's identity was a mystery that gnawed at Zephyrus. Was XOXO an alien from Earth's distant past and future, or was it Zephyrus himself, operating under a different name, Momo, across the temporal expanse? The answers were elusive, slipping through his grasp just as he felt close to understanding them.

"Zephyrus," XOXO's voice echoed in his mind, both familiar and strange. "Our paths are intertwined in ways you have yet to comprehend. The Hyperverse allows us to be in many places at once, to communicate across time and space. This is how it works."

Zephyrus nodded, though the ambiguity of XOXO's words left him with more questions than answers. He knew one thing for certain: the Hyperverse was a conduit, a bridge connecting his present self to XOXO, whether that entity was his future incarnation or something entirely different.

Rhys had become a constant companion on these journeys. Their bond was unshakable, forged in the fires of countless adventures. Yet, there was a new dynamic at play. Rhys and Elara, once close friends to Zephyrus, had found a deeper connection with each other, a bond that had grown while Zephyrus and Elara's relationship had evolved into something different, marked by their experiences in the Hyperverse.

Zephyrus watched as Rhys and Elara conversed, their laughter and shared glances a testament to their growing affection. Despite his initial reservations, Zephyrus had come to accept and even appreciate this new dynamic. His feelings for Elara had shifted, and he found solace in the knowledge that their paths had diverged for a reason.

"Rhys," Zephyrus called out, breaking the serene moment between his friends. "We need to discuss our next move."

Rhys turned, his expression earnest. "What's on your mind, Zephyrus?"

"XOXO," Zephyrus replied. "The more I communicate with him, the more I realize how little I understand. He claims to be an alien from both the past and future, but I can't shake the feeling that he might be me—or a version of me—in the future. He uses the Hyperverse to communicate, and I need to figure out why."

Elara joined the conversation, her gaze thoughtful. "The Hyperverse is a place where time and identity are fluid. It's possible that XOXO is a future you, operating under the name Momo. But why the secrecy?"

Zephyrus sighed, frustration creeping into his voice. "That's what we need to find out. XOXO's messages are always cryptic, filled with hints but never clear answers. We need to delve deeper into the Hyperverse, to find the connections that will reveal the truth."

Rhys nodded, his determination evident. "Then let's do it. We'll explore the Hyperverse and uncover the secrets of XOXO. Whatever the truth is, we'll face it together."

With their course set, they activated the portal device, its energies humming as it connected them to the vast expanse of the Hyperverse. They stepped through, feeling the familiar pull as they were transported to a place where reality bent and twisted, where time was a malleable concept.

They found themselves in a realm of floating islands, each one a different fragment of reality. The sky above was a swirl of colors, constantly shifting and changing. It was a place that defied the conventional laws of physics, a perfect representation of the Hyperverse's boundless potential.

"Where do we start?" Rhys asked, looking around at the surreal landscape.

Zephyrus closed his eyes, focusing on the subtle vibrations of the Hyperverse. "We need to find a place where the past and future converge. XOXO communicates across time, so we need to be somewhere that facilitates that kind of interaction."

They began to explore the floating islands, each one a unique world with its own rules and characteristics. On one island, they found a city frozen in time, its inhabitants locked in a moment of perpetual motion. On another, they encountered a forest where the trees whispered secrets of long-forgotten eras.

As they ventured deeper, they came across an island unlike any other. It was a massive crystal structure, its surface shimmering with an inner light that seemed to pulse in time with the rhythm of the Hyperverse. Zephyrus felt a connection to this place, a resonance that called to him.

"This is it," Zephyrus said, his voice filled with certainty. "This is where we'll find our answers."

The crystal structure had an entrance, a large archway that glowed softly. As they stepped through, they found themselves in a vast chamber filled with intricate machinery and crystalline constructs. The air was charged with energy, a palpable sense of power that flowed through the room.

In the center of the chamber stood a large crystalline device, its surface covered in complex runes and symbols. Zephyrus approached it, feeling a sense of recognition. This device was connected to the Hyperverse, a tool that could bridge the gap between past and future.

"This device," Zephyrus murmured, "it feels like it's tied to XOXO. Maybe it's a way to communicate with him more directly."

Elara examined the runes closely. "These symbols are similar to the ones we've seen in other parts of the Hyperverse. They represent time and space, connection and identity. If we can activate this device, we might be able to reach XOXO."

With a combination of their knowledge and intuition, they began to work on the device. The runes glowed brighter as they made adjustments, the energy in the room intensifying. Finally, with a surge of power, the device activated, creating a swirling vortex of light in the center of the chamber.

From within the vortex, a figure began to form. It was both familiar and alien, a shifting presence that seemed to exist in multiple times at once. Zephyrus felt his heart race as he recognized the form of XOXO.

"Zephyrus," XOXO's voice echoed through the chamber, resonating with a strange harmony. "You have done well to reach this place."

"XOXO," Zephyrus called out, his voice steady despite the whirlwind of emotions. "We need answers. Are you me from the future? Why the secrecy? Why the cryptic messages?"

XOXO's form flickered, a smile playing across its ever-changing features. "The answers you seek are both simple and complex. Yes, I am you, Zephyrus, but also more than that. I am a version of you from a future where identity and time have become fluid. I operate under the name Momo in that future, a name that signifies a new beginning."

Rhys stepped forward, his curiosity evident. "Why the secrecy? Why not just tell us everything directly?"

XOXO's gaze shifted to Rhys, a hint of amusement in his eyes. "The Hyperverse is a place of infinite possibilities. Direct answers can limit those possibilities, closing off paths that might lead to greater understanding. By being cryptic, I encourage you to explore, to discover, and to understand on your own terms."

Elara nodded, understanding dawning on her face. "You wanted us to grow, to learn for ourselves rather than just follow instructions. It's a way of ensuring we truly comprehend the complexities of the Hyperverse."

"Precisely," XOXO affirmed. "You have already shown great wisdom and resilience. But there is still much to learn, many paths to explore. Your journey is far from over."

Zephyrus felt a sense of clarity. "We're ready to continue. We'll face whatever challenges come our way, and we'll uncover the deeper truths of the Hyperverse."

XOXO's form began to fade, the light of the vortex dimming. "Remember, Zephyrus, Rhys, Elara. The Hyperverse is a place of infinite connections. Trust in yourselves and in each other. Your paths will lead you to the understanding you seek."

As XOXO vanished, the chamber returned to its previous state, the energy still humming with potential. Zephyrus turned to his friends, a newfound determination in his eyes. "We have our answers, but our journey continues. There's so much more to discover."

Rhys and Elara nodded, their expressions filled with resolve. "Let's keep exploring," Rhys said. "We'll navigate the Hyperverse together, uncovering its secrets and maintaining the balance."

With their purpose renewed, they set off once more into the vast expanse of the Hyperverse. They encountered new realms, each one a unique tapestry of possibilities. They navigated through landscapes of pure energy, oceans of liquid light, and cities suspended in the void of space.

In one realm, they found a library that contained the collective knowledge of countless civilizations, its shelves filled with books that wrote themselves as they were read. In another, they discovered a temple where the past, present, and future existed simultaneously, each moment a facet of an intricate jewel.

Throughout their journey, Zephyrus continued to communicate with XOXO, now understanding the true nature of their connection. The insights provided by his future self were invaluable, guiding them through the challenges and mysteries of the Hyperverse.

But it wasn't just XOXO who guided them. Zephyrus, Rhys, and Elara relied on each other, their bond growing stronger with each passing day. They faced trials that tested their courage, wisdom, and compassion, emerging from each one with a sense of uncertainty.

Zephyrus felt the weight of the Hyperverse pressing down on him, an infinite expanse of possibilities and challenges that seemed to stretch beyond comprehension. The minions—those entities who inhabited the various realms and often served as guides or obstacles—were increasingly a source of frustration for him. Their cryptic messages and enigmatic behavior only added to the complexity of his journey, making it difficult to discern helpful insights from mere distractions.

"I can't stand these minions," Zephyrus muttered to himself as he navigated yet another convoluted path. "Their riddles and games are just making everything more complicated."

Rhys, sensing his friend's frustration, tried to offer some solace. "I know it's tough, Zephyrus, but sometimes their cryptic ways have hidden meanings. We just need to be patient and look deeper."

Elara, ever the voice of reason, added, "Remember, the Hyperverse is not supposed to be easy. It challenges us so that we can grow and understand it better. Even the minions have their role in this grand design."

Zephyrus sighed, his shoulders slumping slightly. "I know you're both right. It's just... exhausting. Every step forward feels like two steps back because of them."

Their current path led them to a forest of luminescent trees, their branches glowing with a soft, otherworldly light. The air was filled with the hum of unseen energies, and the ground beneath their feet seemed to pulse with a gentle rhythm. It was beautiful, but the beauty was marred by Zephyrus's growing irritation.

Suddenly, a minion appeared before them—a small, ethereal creature with wings that shimmered like starlight. It fluttered around them, its voice a melodic whisper. "Seekers of the Hyperverse, you have come far, but the path ahead is fraught with peril. Only those who understand the dance of light and shadow may proceed."

Zephyrus groaned inwardly. "Great, another riddle."

Rhys stepped forward, trying to engage the minion. "Can you give us more specific guidance? We're trying to understand the Hyperverse and our place within it."

The minion's eyes sparkled with an amused glint. "Specific guidance is found within the heart of the riddle. Light and shadow are but two sides of the same coin. Embrace both, and you shall see the way."

As the minion fluttered away, leaving behind a trail of shimmering light, Zephyrus clenched his fists. "See what I mean? How are we supposed to make sense of that?"

Elara placed a reassuring hand on his shoulder. "We'll figure it out together, Zephyrus. We've faced tougher challenges before. Let's think about what the minion said."

They sat down beneath one of the luminescent trees, its light casting a calming glow over them. Zephyrus closed his eyes, trying to clear his mind and focus on the riddle. "Light and shadow... two sides of the same coin. What could that mean?"

Rhys, deep in thought, spoke up. "Maybe it's about balance. The Hyperverse is all about balance, right? Light and shadow could symbolize different aspects of that balance."

Elara nodded. "That makes sense. We need to find a way to balance these elements, to see the path ahead more clearly."

Zephyrus opened his eyes, a spark of determination reigniting within him. "Alright, let's look for places where light and shadow interact. Maybe there's something we're missing."

They continued their journey through the forest, paying close attention to the interplay of light and shadow. The trees cast intricate patterns on the ground, creating areas of darkness amidst the glow. It was in one of these shadowed areas that they noticed something peculiar—a small, stone pedestal with an inscription etched into its surface.

Rhys knelt down to read the inscription. "In the dance of light and shadow, the truth shall be revealed. Embrace both, and the path will open."

Zephyrus felt a flicker of hope. "This must be it. We need to activate this pedestal somehow."

Elara examined the pedestal closely. "There are grooves here, like something needs to be placed in them. Maybe we need to create a balance of light and shadow."

They gathered materials from the forest—glowing crystals from the trees and stones from the shadowed areas. Carefully, they placed the crystals and stones into the grooves on the pedestal, arranging them to create a balance of light and dark.

As the last piece was set into place, the pedestal began to glow, and a doorway of light and shadow materialized before them. Zephyrus felt a surge of triumph. "We did it! The path is open."

They stepped through the doorway, finding themselves in a new realm that was both awe-inspiring and daunting. The landscape was a mosaic of floating islands, each one a different world with its own unique characteristics. Some islands were bathed in brilliant light, while others were shrouded in deep shadow.

A voice echoed through the realm, calm and serene. "Welcome, seekers. You have passed the first test of balance. Continue forward, and you will find what you seek."

Zephyrus felt a mixture of relief and determination. "Let's keep going. We're on the right track."

As they navigated the floating islands, the interplay of light and shadow became more pronounced. They encountered challenges that required them to think creatively and work together, using their understanding of balance to overcome obstacles.

On one island, they faced a labyrinth made of mirrored walls that reflected light in confusing patterns. They had to find their way through by carefully observing the reflections and identifying the true path amidst the illusions.

Rhys, his analytical mind at work, suggested, "Look for the reflections that don't quite match up. Those might be the clues we need."

Elara agreed. "And we should use the shadows to our advantage. They might reveal hidden passages."

Their combined efforts paid off, and they navigated the labyrinth successfully. At its center, they found a crystal orb that radiated both light and shadow, a symbol of the balance they sought.

The orb's light coalesced into a figure—another minion, but this one exuded an air of ancient wisdom. "You have done well to reach this point. The path ahead requires you to trust in your instincts and each other. The journey is as important as the destination."

Zephyrus couldn't help but feel a grudging respect for the minions. Despite their cryptic nature, they were guiding them in ways he hadn't fully appreciated before. "Thank you," he said, his voice sincere.

As they moved forward, the challenges grew more intricate, but their confidence and unity grew stronger. They found themselves relying on each other's strengths more than ever before, understanding that their differences were what made them a formidable team.

At one point, they encountered a chasm that seemed impossible to cross. The edges were shrouded in darkness, while the center glowed with an intense, blinding light. Zephyrus realized that they needed to create a bridge of balance, using both light and shadow to traverse the gap.

"Let's use the glowing crystals and the shadow stones again," Zephyrus suggested. "We can create a pathway that balances both elements."

With careful precision, they constructed a bridge of alternating light and dark, the stones fitting together like pieces of a puzzle. As they stepped onto the bridge, it held firm, carrying them safely to the other side.

Their final challenge brought them to a temple at the heart of the realm, a place where light and shadow merged in a dance of harmony. The temple's entrance was guarded by a figure that seemed to be made of both light and shadow, its form shifting between the two states.

"To enter the temple," the guardian intoned, "you must prove that you understand the true nature of balance. Show me that you can embrace both light and shadow within yourselves."

Zephyrus stepped forward, his voice resolute. "We have faced many challenges to get here. We have learned to balance light and shadow, to understand that both are essential to the harmony of the Hyperverse."

Rhys and Elara joined him, their expressions reflecting the same determination. "We are ready," Rhys said. "We will embrace both aspects to prove our understanding."

The guardian's eyes glowed with approval. "Very well. Show me."

In a moment of unity, they focused on the lessons they had learned, allowing themselves to feel both the light of their hopes and the shadows of their fears. They reached out to each other, their hands clasping in a circle of solidarity.

As they did so, the guardian's form stabilized, becoming a harmonious blend of light and shadow. "You have proven your understanding. Enter the temple, and may you find the wisdom you seek."

The temple doors opened, revealing a sanctuary filled with symbols of balance—yin and yang, sun and moon, day and night. At the center of the sanctuary was a crystal pedestal, similar to the one they had encountered in the forest but more intricate and radiant.

Approaching the pedestal, they saw an inscription that read, "To understand the Hyperverse, one must see beyond the duality of light and shadow, to the unity that lies beneath."

Zephyrus placed his hand on the pedestal, feeling a surge of energy course through him. Visions filled his mind, showing him the interconnectedness of all things within the Hyperverse. He saw the paths of countless beings, each one a thread in the intricate tapestry of existence.

Rhys and Elara experienced similar visions, their understanding deepening as they saw the balance and unity that underpinned the Hyperverse. The knowledge they gained was profound, a testament to the journey they had undertaken.

As the visions faded, Zephyrus felt a sense of peace and clarity. "We have learned so much, but there is still more to discover. The Hyperverse is infinite, and expanding.

The vapeware they all used had an origin far removed from the extraordinary experiences they were having in the Hyperverse. Initially developed as a dissociative anesthetic, its primary purpose was to provide a safe, controlled environment for patients undergoing surgery. However, in the hands of those who sought to explore the boundaries of consciousness and reality, it had revealed far more. Zephyrus and his companions had discovered that this vapeware had the ability to elucidate alien intrusion on Earth, bringing to light entities and influences that had previously gone unnoticed.

As Zephyrus stood in the heart of the temple, he couldn't shake the sense of disbelief that lingered in his mind. The challenges they faced, the paths they navigated, all seemed too intricately designed to be mere coincidence. Even though he knew he was part of something greater, a participant in the vast interconnected web of the Hyperverse, he found it hard to believe that he could have planned any of this without remembering. It was as if he was watching someone else's life unfold through a distorted lens, uncertain if it was truly his own actions he was witnessing.

"It's still so surreal," Zephyrus murmured to himself. "To think that I might have orchestrated all this... it doesn't feel like it's me. How can I be sure of anything in this place?"

The echoes of his thoughts were interrupted by a gentle voice in his mind, the familiar presence of XOXO. "Zephyrus, the Hyperverse reflects many possibilities. What you see and experience may not always align with your current understanding of yourself. Trust in the journey and in the knowledge that you are part of a much larger design."

Zephyrus sighed, trying to reconcile his doubts with the wisdom of XOXO. Meanwhile, his thoughts drifted to Baby Morgan, the infant whose presence seemed to pervade their experiences. Baby Morgan was still learning, an innocent being just beginning to grasp the complexities of existence. When this small child manipulated the minions, they, too, exhibited an infantile nature, mirroring the learning and growth process of their young master.

Rhys and Elara noticed Zephyrus's contemplative state and approached him with concern. "Zephyrus," Elara said softly, "we're all feeling the weight of this journey. It's natural to have doubts, but we need to keep moving forward. The answers will come."

Rhys added, "We're in this together. The vapeware has shown us things we never imagined, but it's also brought us closer to understanding the true nature of the Hyperverse. We just need to keep our minds open."

Zephyrus nodded, grateful for their support. "You're right. We need to keep exploring, keep seeking the truth. The Hyperverse has many layers, and we're just beginning to peel them back."

As they continued their journey, they found themselves in a region of the Hyperverse that was strikingly different from anything they had encountered before. The landscape was a series of floating platforms connected by translucent bridges, each platform housing intricate machinery and enigmatic symbols. The air was thick with a shimmering mist, giving everything an ethereal quality.

On one of the platforms, they encountered a group of minions that appeared even more infantile than those they had seen before. These minions were small, with round, wide-eyed faces and a curious demeanor. They moved about clumsily, as if still learning how to interact with their environment.

One of the minions approached Zephyrus, holding out a small, glowing orb. "Seekers, this is a gift from Baby Morgan. It will help you understand more about the nature of the Hyperverse."

Zephyrus took the orb, feeling a gentle warmth radiate from it. "Thank you. We'll use this wisely."

As they examined the orb, it began to project images and symbols, each one offering insights into the workings of the Hyperverse. They saw depictions of various entities, including aliens who had interacted with Earth throughout history. These aliens had used advanced technology and consciousness manipulation to influence human development, often going unnoticed by the broader population.

Elara studied the images intently. "This explains so much. The vapeware isn't just a tool for consciousness exploration; it's a bridge to these alien influences. It's how we've been able to see and interact with them."

Rhys agreed. "And it makes sense why Baby Morgan and the minions exhibit such an infantile nature. They're still learning, just like we are. Their actions are guided by curiosity and the need to understand."

Zephyrus felt a renewed sense of purpose. "If Baby Morgan and the minions are still learning, then we have a responsibility to guide them, just as we seek guidance from XOXO and the other entities we've encountered. This journey is about mutual growth and understanding."

With this realization, they set out to explore the floating platforms, using the orb's projections to guide them. Each platform revealed more about the intricate connections within the Hyperverse, showing them how different beings and realities intersected.

At one point, they came across a platform with a large, crystalline structure at its center. The structure pulsed with energy, its surface covered in complex runes that seemed to shift and change as they watched. Zephyrus approached it cautiously, feeling a strong sense of familiarity.

"This structure... it feels like it's connected to the Nexus of Echoes," Zephyrus said, his voice filled with awe. "It's like a focal point for the energies of the Hyperverse."

Elara nodded. "I think you're right. If we can understand how this structure works, we might be able to gain deeper insights into the nature of the Hyperverse and our own paths within it."

They began to study the runes, using the knowledge they had gained from the orb and their previous experiences. As they worked, they noticed patterns emerging, connections that linked the structure to the various realms they had explored.

Rhys pointed to a series of runes that glowed with a faint blue light. "These runes seem to correspond to the different realities we've encountered. If we can activate them in the right sequence, we might be able to unlock new pathways within the Hyperverse."

With careful precision, they activated the runes, each one lighting up in response to their touch. As the final rune was activated, the structure began to hum with energy, and a portal opened at its center.

Stepping through the portal, they found themselves in a realm of breathtaking beauty. The landscape was a vibrant tapestry of colors and shapes, constantly shifting and evolving. In the distance, they saw a massive tree with crystalline branches that seemed to stretch into infinity.

"This place is incredible," Elara whispered, her voice filled with wonder. "It's like a living representation of the Hyperverse."

As they approached the tree, they noticed that its branches were adorned with countless orbs, each one glowing with a unique light. Zephyrus reached out to touch one of the orbs, feeling a surge of energy as it responded to his presence.

The orb projected an image of a young child—Baby Morgan—playing with minions in a field of flowers. The scene was filled with laughter and joy, a stark contrast to the challenges they had faced. It was a reminder of the innocence and wonder that lay at the heart of their journey.

Rhys watched the projection, a smile spreading across his face. "It's easy to forget that amidst all the complexity, there's still a core of simplicity and joy. Baby Morgan is still learning, just like we are."

Elara added, "And the minions, despite their infantile nature, are an essential part of this learning process. They're not just obstacles; they're fellow travelers on this journey."

Zephyrus felt a deep sense of connection to the scene before him. "We need to remember that we're all part of the same tapestry. The Hyperverse challenges us, but it also teaches us. We just need to be open to its lessons."

As they continued to explore the realm, they encountered other beings—some familiar, others entirely new. Each encounter added to their understanding, revealing new facets of the Hyperverse and their own roles within it.

At one point, they came across a group of beings that appeared to be made of pure light. These beings communicated through a series of melodic tones, their voices blending together in a harmonious symphony.

One of the light beings approached them, its tones resonating with a sense of welcome. "Travelers, you have come far. We are the Luminara, guardians of the Tree of Realities. You seek knowledge and understanding, and we can help you."

Zephyrus bowed respectfully. "Thank you, Luminara. We seek to understand the true nature of the Hyperverse and our place within it."

The Luminara's tones shifted, conveying a sense of approval. "You have shown great wisdom and perseverance. The Tree of Realities holds many secrets, and we will guide you to those that you are ready to comprehend."

With the Luminara's guidance, they explored the Tree of Realities, each branch and orb revealing new insights and connections. They learned about the cycles of creation and destruction that governed the Hyperverse, the interplay of light and shadow, and the delicate balance that maintained the harmony of all realities.

Through their journey, Zephyrus's doubts began to fade. He realized that the minions, the challenges, and the cryptic messages were all part of a larger design, a tapestry that was as intricate as it was beautiful. The Hyperverse was a place of infinite possibilities, and each step they took brought them closer to understanding its true nature.

As they stood beneath the Tree of Realities, Zephyrus felt a sense of peace and clarity. "We have come so far, and yet our journey is just beginning. The Hyperverse is infinite, and there is still so much to learn. But with the knowledge we've gained and the bonds we've forged, I know we can face whatever challenges lie ahead."

The loop continues, an endless cycle of discovery and challenge, as Zephyrus and his companions navigate the vast and enigmatic Hyperverse. Each step brings them closer to understanding, yet the path stretches infinitely before them. The deeper they delve, the more they realize the intricate interplay of forces at work, both within the Hyperverse and back on Earth.

The realization hits Zephyrus one night as they camp beneath the branches of the Tree of Realities. The vapeware they use is not just a tool for exploring consciousness; it is a means of control. The aliens, whose presence they had begun to glimpse through the veil of the Hyperverse, use these drugs to manipulate the minds of mortals on Earth. This revelation is as disturbing as it is enlightening, shedding new light on their journey.

"These drugs," Zephyrus murmured, staring into the fire, "they're not just opening doors to new experiences. They're allowing alien forces to control us, to bend our wills to their purposes."

Rhys, seated next to him, frowned thoughtfully. "But why? What's their endgame? Why go to such lengths to control humanity?"

Elara, always the voice of reason, leaned forward. "Control over a species, especially one as adaptable and resourceful as humans, could give them significant influence over the development of Earth. If they can manipulate our thoughts and actions, they can shape our future to their advantage."

Zephyrus nodded, feeling the weight of this new understanding. "And Momo—my future self, or whatever he truly is—seems to be manipulating time itself to create the Hyperverse on Earth. It's all connected. The drugs, the aliens, Momo's interventions—they're all part of the same web."

The next morning, they set out with renewed determination. Their journey took them to a realm where time seemed to flow differently, a place where the past, present, and future overlapped in a continuous loop. It was here, they believed, that they could find more clues about Momo's tampering and the true nature of the Hyperverse.

As they explored this temporal nexus, they encountered scenes from their own lives, moments that had already passed and others that had yet to occur. Each scene was a piece of a larger puzzle, a clue to understanding the machinations at play.

In one such scene, Zephyrus saw himself as a child, playing with a toy spaceship in the garden of his childhood home. The simplicity of the moment was jarring against the backdrop of their current struggles, a reminder of the innocence they had lost.

"I remember this day," Zephyrus said softly. "It was before everything changed, before I started to see the world differently."

Rhys placed a reassuring hand on his shoulder. "These memories are part of who you are, Zephyrus. They shape you, just as your actions shape the future."

Elara, watching the scene, added, "And it's not just your past that matters. The future you're working towards is just as important. We need to understand Momo's plans, to see how they fit into this larger picture."

Their exploration led them to a chamber filled with intricate machinery, devices that seemed to hum with the energy of the Hyperverse. At the center of the chamber stood a console covered in symbols and runes, a control panel that appeared to be linked to the flow of time itself.

"This must be it," Zephyrus said, approaching the console with a mix of awe and apprehension. "This is where Momo's been tampering with time, creating the Hyperverse on Earth."

Rhys examined the runes closely. "If we can decipher these symbols, we might be able to understand what Momo's doing and how to counteract it."

Elara nodded. "Let's get to work. We need to understand this technology if we're going to stop the manipulation and set things right."

As they worked, deciphering the complex runes and symbols, they began to piece together the nature of Momo's interventions. He was using the Hyperverse as a tool to manipulate events on Earth, creating a version of reality that suited his own purposes. By altering key moments in time, he was shaping the development of humanity, guiding it along a path that aligned with his vision.

"This is incredible," Rhys said, his voice filled with a mix of admiration and horror. "He's altering history itself, creating a hyperverse on Earth that's molded to his will."

Zephyrus felt a surge of determination. "We need to find a way to stop this. We can't let Momo, or whoever he truly is, control our destiny like this."

Their efforts began to pay off as they unraveled the workings of the console. They discovered a way to trace Momo's interventions, to follow the threads of his manipulations through time. It was a daunting task, but they knew it was the key to understanding and ultimately stopping his plans.

As they delved deeper, they encountered more scenes from their own lives, each one a piece of the puzzle. They saw moments where their paths had been subtly altered, decisions influenced by forces beyond their control. It was a sobering realization, but it also strengthened their resolve.

"We need to be vigilant," Elara said. "We can't let these manipulations define us. We have to take control of our own destinies."

Zephyrus nodded. "And we need to find Momo. If we can confront him, maybe we can understand his true motives and put an end to this."

Their journey through the temporal nexus took them to a place where time itself seemed to converge, a singularity where all moments intersected. It was here that they felt Momo's presence most strongly, a tangible force that seemed to pulse with the energy of the Hyperverse.

"He's here," Zephyrus said, his voice barely a whisper. "This is where it all converges."

As they approached the singularity, the air around them shimmered with a strange, almost electric energy. They felt a pull, as if they were being drawn into the very fabric of time itself. It was a disorienting sensation, but they pressed on, driven by the need to understand and confront Momo.

At the heart of the singularity, they found a figure standing amidst the swirling energies. It was Momo, his form both familiar and alien, a reflection of Zephyrus yet something entirely different.

"Zephyrus," Momo said, his voice a resonant echo. "You have come far. I have been waiting for this moment."

Zephyrus felt a mix of emotions—anger, confusion, and a strange sense of kinship. "Momo, or whatever you truly are, why are you doing this? Why manipulate time and create the Hyperverse on Earth?"

Momo's eyes gleamed with a complex emotion. "I am you, and yet I am more. I have seen the infinite possibilities of the Hyperverse, the countless paths humanity can take. My actions are meant to guide, to create a reality that is more harmonious, more advanced."

Rhys stepped forward, his expression determined. "But you're taking away our free will. You're shaping our destiny without our consent."

Momo nodded slowly. "I understand your concern, but my actions are not without purpose. The Hyperverse is a place of infinite possibilities, and without guidance, those possibilities can lead to chaos."

Elara's voice was firm. "There must be another way. We can work together to find a balance, to ensure that humanity's path is guided but not controlled."

Momo considered their words, a flicker of uncertainty crossing his face. "Perhaps you are right. Perhaps there is a way to guide without controlling, to influence without dictating."

Zephyrus felt a glimmer of hope. "We can find that way together. The Hyperverse is vast, and there is much we still need to understand. But we can do it, as equals."

For a moment, the singularity pulsed with a bright light, the energies around them harmonizing. Momo's form seemed to stabilize, becoming more human, more like Zephyrus.

"Very well," Momo said, his voice softer. "Let us find that balance. Together, we can explore the Hyperverse and guide humanity's path without taking away its freedom."

With this newfound understanding, Zephyrus, Rhys, Elara, and Momo began to work together. They used the console to trace and adjust the threads of time, ensuring that humanity's development was influenced but not controlled. It was a delicate balance, but one they were determined to maintain.

Their journey continued, each step bringing new challenges and revelations. They encountered more aliens, beings who had their own agendas and influences on Earth. They learned to navigate these interactions, using their understanding of the Hyperverse to maintain the balance.

As they traveled, they also continued to guide Baby Morgan, helping the infant learn and grow. They understood that Baby Morgan's innocence and curiosity were vital to their journey, a reminder of the simplicity and wonder at the heart of the Hyperverse.

Through their efforts, they began to see the fruits of their labor. The Hyperverse became a place of harmony, a realm where different beings and realities coexisted in balance. Humanity's path was guided but free, shaped by both internal and external influences yet ultimately determined by its own choices.

Zephyrus felt a deep sense of fulfillment. "We've come so far, and yet there's still so much to learn. The Hyperverse is infinite, and our journey is never truly over. But with each step, we grow stronger, wiser, and more connected."

Rhys and Elara stood by his side, their faces reflecting the same determination and hope. "We'll continue this journey together," Rhys said. "And we'll face whatever challenges come our way."

As they looked out over the vast expanse of the Hyperverse, they knew that their journey was just beginning. The loop continued, each cycle a wrap around.

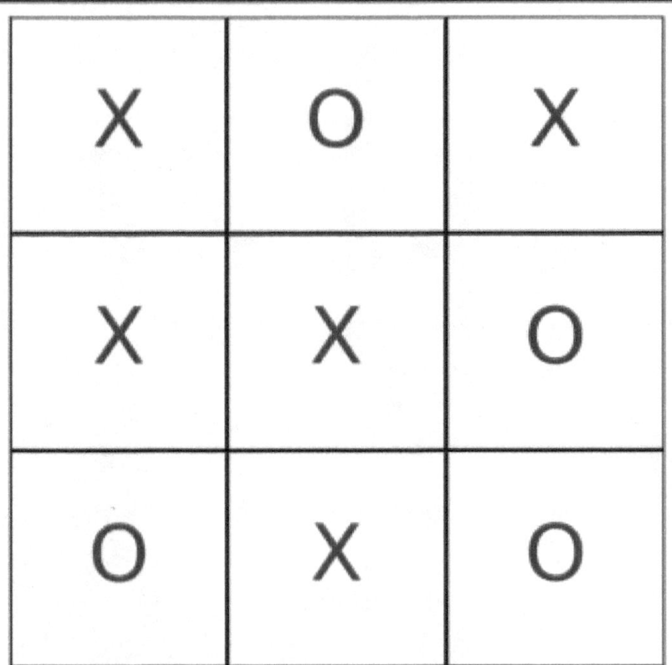

THE CHRONICLES OF ZEPHYRUS
GARTH TOXO